There was a possibility that this child was his...

Ryan's first step was to convince Delaney to do the DNA test. The doors of his heart seemed to be opening, and Ryan had no idea how or why they were doing that. Or if he could even close them again. He took a few steps closer toward Delaney and stopped. It was best to keep some physical distance between them since he wasn't doing great in the emotional distance department.

"I got some news. The New Hope Clinic was located in the hospital where my son died." Thankfully he'd managed to lay that out without too much emotion in his voice.

Still holding her son, Delaney made a sound of contemplation. "It doesn't prove anything."

Ryan turned his head in the baby's direction and just like that, their gazes connected. His hair was blond. He kicked his chubby legs and grinned.

Ryan's breath froze in his lungs. He couldn't move. Couldn't speak. Because he knew...

PEEKABOO BABY
DELORES FOSSEN

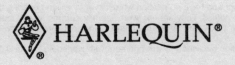

HARLEQUIN®

TORONTO • NEW YORK • LONDON
AMSTERDAM • PARIS • SYDNEY • HAMBURG
STOCKHOLM • ATHENS • TOKYO • MILAN • MADRID
PRAGUE • WARSAW • BUDAPEST • AUCKLAND

ISBN 0-373-88643-8

PEEKABOO BABY

Copyright © 2005 by Delores Fossen

This edition published by arrangement with Harlequin Books S.A.

® and TM are trademarks of the publisher. Trademarks indicated with ® are registered in the United States Patent and Trademark Office, the Canadian Trade Marks Office and in other countries.

www.eHarlequin.com

Printed in U.S.A.

ABOUT THE AUTHOR

Imagine a family tree that includes Texas cowboys, Choctaw and Cherokee Indians, a Louisiana pirate and a Scottish rebel who battled side by side with William Wallace. With ancestors like that, it's easy to understand why Texas author and former U.S. Air Force captain Delores Fossen feels as if she was genetically predisposed to writing romances. Along the way to fulfilling her DNA destiny, Delores married an Air Force Top Gun who just happens to be of Viking descent. With all those romantic bases covered, she doesn't have to look too far for inspiration.

Books by Delores Fossen

HARLEQUIN INTRIGUE

Don't miss any of our special offers. Write to us at the following address for information on our newest releases.

Harlequin Reader Service
U.S.: 3010 Walden Ave., P.O. Box 1325, Buffalo, NY 14269
Canadian: P.O. Box 609, Fort Erie, Ont. L2A 5X3

CAST OF CHARACTERS

Delaney Nash—Could the donor embryo she used to give birth to her son, Patrick, be the cloned son of her enemy, Ryan McCall? Now, to keep her son safe, Delaney has to turn to this man she fears could ultimately claim her child, and her heart.

Ryan McCall—Desperate for a second chance to raise his son, Ryan is willing to do whatever it takes to keep Delaney and their baby safe. But risking his heart is something he never expected.

Patrick Nash—The child Delaney always desperately wanted and the son Ryan thought he'd lost. But will Ryan lose Patrick again, this time to a killer?

Dr. Emmett Montgomery—Director of the New Hope fertility clinic and the man who possibly wants to cover up what happened with Delaney's donor embryo.

Richard Nash—Delaney's father. Is he so obsessed with getting revenge against Ryan and Delaney that he's willing to commit murder?

Dr. Bryson Keyes—Delaney's doctor. He possibly performed illegal cloning experiments that resulted in Patrick's birth. Now he might want to eliminate any evidence of those experiments, including Ryan, Delaney and Patrick.

Chapter One

San Antonio, Texas

Looking through her rain-spattered windshield, Delaney Nash spotted Dr. Bryson Keyes in the doorway of the private entrance of the New Hope clinic.

Finally.

Soon she'd get answers about what had possibly happened to her son. If Dr. Keyes or one of his associates had done something to harm him...

But she couldn't even finish that thought.

Her baby had to be all right.

He just had to be.

Delaney blinked back the tears she'd been fighting and watched as Dr. Keyes popped open his oversize charcoal-gray umbrella. Ducking his head against the gusty April wind, he stepped out into the rain and walked toward his car in his personalized space of the parking lot. No doubt his daily routine. Except there was nothing routine about today.

The doctor hadn't changed much in the thirteen months since she'd last seen him. The same lanky build. The same receding orangy-red hair. Of course, now there was something disturbing about him. But before the questions, before the allegations, Dr. Bryson Keyes had simply been the fertility specialist who'd given her a son, Patrick.

A miracle.

Now, she had to wonder if that miracle was about to become a nightmare.

Delaney got out of her own car, hurrying, and under the meager cover of her own umbrella, she followed Dr. Keyes across the parking lot. The wind and drizzle picked up speed and spit at her, splattering her caramel-colored skirt and probably ruining it in the process. It didn't matter. Besides, it was a small price to pay to rid her of the questions and doubts that had been tormenting her for the past forty-eight hours.

The thought of the possible answers to those questions knotted her stomach. Again. It caused her heart to slam hard against her chest, and it robbed her of her already too-thin breath. Delaney choked back the worst-case scenarios that kept racing through her head and instead used her determined stride to eat up the distance between Dr. Keyes and her.

Her footsteps, or maybe something else, alerted him, because his head whipped up, and he spun around to face her. His entire body seemed to go stiff, and his watery blue eyes widened with what appeared to be a combination of recognition and concern.

"Ms. Nash," he said, his words muted because of the relentless slapping of rain on their umbrellas.

"Dr. Keyes." It took Delaney several moments to tamp down the emotion just so she could speak. "I've been trying to get in touch with you for the past two days."

He slipped his hand into his jacket pocket and extracted his keys. He checked his watch and gave an impatient glance around the parking lot. "I've been busy, and unfortunately I don't have time to see you now. You can call my office and make an appointment."

And with that cool, attempted dismissal, the doctor turned to leave. But that wasn't going to happen. Not until she'd gotten what she came for. Delaney latched on to his arm and held on as if he were her last hope.

Which unfortunately wasn't too far from the truth.

"I've already tried to make an appointment. Several times. Your office claimed you were booked solid," Delaney accused. "And I don't think it's my imagination that you're trying to avoid me. Guess what? It won't work."

He didn't deny the part about avoiding her. Nor did he offer any polite excuse for why he hadn't responded to the dozen or so frantic messages she'd left with his secretary and answering service. What he did do was look again uneasily around the parking lot.

"This isn't a good place to talk," he informed her.

It was a dismissal, one that riled Delaney to the core, and he no doubt would have left it at that if she hadn't dug her fingers into his arm and held on. "This might not be a good place to talk, but it'll have to do. Neither of us is leaving until you explain why a representative from a medical watchdog group—Physicians Against Unethical Practices—called me."

Oh, that stopped him cold.

Dead cold.

Dr. Keyes met her gaze head-on. Gone were the dismissals and the annoyance at her interruption, and Delaney thought she saw some fear.

An emotion she totally understood.

Because she was afraid.

Terrified, really.

For her son.

And for what might have already happened to him.

"This group contacted you?" Dr. Keyes asked.

Delaney nodded and tried to keep her voice level. Hard to do with the storm of emotions swirling inside her. "They implied that the New Hope clinic would soon be under federal investigation for some kind of illegal medical practices. Is that true?"

And Delaney held what was left of her

breath. Waiting. Praying. Hoping that Dr. Keyes would deny it or else explain it all away.

That didn't happen.

"What did you tell them?" the doctor demanded, and there was no doubt that his question was a demand. His wiry jaw turned to iron.

"Nothing. Because I don't know anything to tell." She paused a heartbeat. "But it's my guess that you do."

He shrugged, not exactly the declaration of innocence.

Delaney stepped closer, and she was sure her jaw muscles were steely, as well. She also made sure some of that steel crept into her eyes. "Let's take a little trip down memory lane here. Fifteen months ago I came to New Hope when I found out I was infertile. I desperately wanted a baby, and you arranged for a donor embryo. It worked on the first try. I got pregnant, and I delivered my son four months ago."

Because she had no choice, Delaney paused to gather her breath and her courage. Because what she had to say would take every ounce of courage that she could marshal. "Now, I've learned that the clinic might have done something illegal to the embryo that became my son. Maybe some cellular experiments. DNA manipulation—whatever. Something that could perhaps make him sick...or worse."

No amount of strength could have stopped the tears that sprang to her eyes. Hot tears that burned against the cool rain speckling her lashes. Delaney fought the tears, and lost. The fear and dread were overwhelming.

Dr. Keyes or someone else at the clinic might have used her son as a guinea pig, and those experiments might have irreversible long-term effects.

"I have to think about this," Dr. Keyes said. He gestured toward his car. "I'll be in touch."

Delaney caught the front of his jacket and wadded up the fabric so she had a firm grip. "You'll tell me what you know *now,*" she said through clenched teeth. "Did you do something to my son?"

He mumbled something under his breath. Cursed. And looked as if he would prefer to be in the deepest pit of hell rather than talking to her.

Seconds crawled by, with the rain pelting them, and Delaney wasn't sure the doctor would even answer her. She had no idea what she would do if he didn't. Still, she was desperate, and she'd use that desperation to get him to talk.

"Any idea if the watchdog group contacted Ryan McCall as well?" Dr. Keyes asked.

The question caused her stomach to land in the vicinity of her knees.

Of all the things she'd anticipated the doctor might say, that wasn't one of them.

"Ryan McCall?" Delaney managed to repeat. Not easily though. The man's name always seemed to stick like wet clay in her throat. "Why would they contact him about illegal medical practices at the New Hope clinic? He has nothing to do with any of this."

Judging from the panicky stare that Dr. Keyes gave her, and from his suddenly wobbling Adam's apple, he thought differently.

Well, he was wrong.

He *had* to be.

Her old nemesis, Ryan McCall, had no connection to her son. *None.* McCall was a different part of her past. A past she dearly wanted to forget. Of course, forgetting wasn't entirely possible. Every time she heard her father's accusing voice and saw his scarred wrists, she got a harsh reminder that Ryan McCall, one of the most affluent and ruthless businessmen in the state, had tried to destroy her family.

And in many ways, he'd succeeded.

Heck, he was *still* succeeding.

"Look," Dr. Keyes grumbled. "Let's get in my car. It's probably not a good idea for us to stand out here discussing this. The watchdog group employs P.I.s. They could have followed you."

Delaney stayed put. "Answers," she demanded. "Now. And quit stalling."

His suddenly intense, almost angry stare drilled into her. "You're really going to wish you'd sat down for this," Keyes warned, his voice now a dangerous growl.

Delaney wasn't immune to the warning and that stare. Even though she hadn't thought it possible, it sent her adrenaline soaring even higher than it already was. Still, she didn't back down. She couldn't. No matter how painful this was, she had to learn the truth.

"Start talking," Delaney countered, trying to show strength that she in no way felt. Her legs were shaking so hard she was afraid she might lose her balance. "Because if you don't, I'm going straight to the police. I'll demand a full investigation, and I'll tell them to start that investigation with you."

He stared at her. "And if I tell you what you *think* you want to know?"

"Then, it ends here."

She hoped.

Mercy, it had to end here.

Dr. Keyes gave a curt, brace-yourself nod. "I believe an embryologist who used to work at the clinic might have done some experimental research on asexually replicated cells."

Delaney mentally repeated that. She understood the individual words, but the term, asexually replicated cells, meant nothing to her. "Try that again in English."

He opened his mouth and closed it, as if rethinking what he was about to say. Then he shook his head. "The embryologist, William Spears, died about three weeks ago. His records are apparently missing now, and I only got a glimpse of them beforehand, so I'm not exactly sure what he did. I'm not even sure if the embryo you were given was part of his research. In fact, I'm not sure of anything. I only learned what he'd done after he was dead—and that means I'm innocent of any charges this watchdog group might bring against the clinic."

Using the grip she still had on his jacket, Delaney hauled him closer. "Frankly, I don't care what part you had in this. All I care about is my son. I need to make sure he's all right, that someone didn't manipulate or mutate the embryo so that it could end up harming him."

That improved his posture. "Is there something wrong with your son?"

"Not that I know of. That's why I'm here. I want to make sure there's nothing lurking in his DNA that could turn out to be a deadly time bomb."

"No time bomb." More hesitation. Another check around the parking lot. "I don't believe your son's DNA was altered."

The breath of relief instantly formed in her lungs and then stalled there, because that wasn't a relief-generating look on the doctor's face. "Then what did you do to him?"

"Me personally? Nothing." He groaned and kicked at the puddle of rain that was deepening around their feet. "Asexually replicated cells aren't mutated or altered. They're just that—asexually reproduced."

Delaney wished she'd paid more attention in her Biology 101 class at Texas A&M. She shook her head. "I don't understand."

Dr. Keyes lowered his voice to a whisper. "Your son's embryo was cloned."

She pulled in her breath. "Cloned?" The grip she had on the doctor's jacket melted away, and Delaney's hand dropped to her side.

"Yes. I only got a quick look at Dr. Spears's records, but he claims to have taken the DNA from a six-week-old male infant who died two years ago right here in San Antonio in an automobile accident that killed both the baby and his mother."

A sickening feeling of dread came over her.

Two years ago.

A car accident.

A child and mother left dead.

Delaney was positive there'd been plenty of other accidents, other deaths during that time frame. But only one incident came to mind.

"It's possible that you might have received the cloned embryo from that infant," Dr. Keyes said.

Delaney felt herself stagger, and because she had no choice, she leaned against a nearby car.

An experimentally cloned embryo.

The genetic copy of a child who had already been born.

And died.

Delaney tried to respond, tried to question that. She tried to accuse Dr. Keyes of lying. Yes, that was it. He had to be lying. But she couldn't make herself say anything. Her throat clamped shut, and the tightness in her chest squeezed like a fist.

"If the information in that record is correct," the doctor continued. He waited until Delaney's eyes came back to his. "Then, the child you gave birth to is Ryan McCall's son."

Chapter Two

Ryan McCall cursed the storm. It was a brutal reminder of the gaping wound that just wouldn't heal.

The rain had been relentless, going on for hours. And each new assault against the massive floor-to-ceiling windows of his office drew him out of the concentration that he was fighting hard to maintain.

Concentration he desperately needed tonight.

Ryan tried—again—to lose himself in the quarterly business projections for his company, McCall Industries. A vital report. One he needed to absorb and study so he could give input to his department heads. It worked. Well, it worked for a minute or two anyway. And then there was another wave of rain. Another burst of wind.

Another stir of painful memories he didn't want.

It had rained the afternoon of *the* accident two years ago. Violent weather, violent consequences. The connection wasn't logical, but it was there nonetheless. Ryan considered it a battle to fight, and win.

Eventually.

That's why he didn't close the curtains. One way or another, he would conquer this particular demon just as he'd conquered all the others in his life.

The buzzing sound of the intercom echoed through the room only seconds before he heard the familiar voice of his household manager, Lena Sanchez. "Sorry to interrupt you, boss, but you have a visitor at the front gate."

Ryan automatically checked the antique Seth Thomas clock on the polished-stone-and-mahogany mantel. It was just after seven-thirty. Not late, but since his estate wasn't exactly on the beaten path, it was hardly the hour for an unexpected guest. And an unwanted one. Ryan didn't have to know the person's identity to determine that. Anyone was unwanted at this point.

He was not in a receiving-visitors kind of mood.

"It's Delaney Nash," Lena added, sounding concerned. "And she said it's important."

That captured Ryan's attention.

Tossing the report aside, he reached over, accessed the security feed on his computer and zoomed in on the wrought-iron gate that fronted his estate. Even through the thick gray rain and the dusky light, he had no trouble spotting the blue car. Or the woman sitting behind the wheel. Her window was halfway down, and she was staring blankly at the intercom and security camera, apparently waiting for Lena to open the gate so she could *visit*.

Even though Ryan knew her name as well as his own, he'd yet to meet Delaney Nash, the woman he'd spoken to and corresponded with too many times to count. That didn't mean he wanted their first meeting to happen tonight. Still, there was something about her ashen face and shell-shocked stare that had him reconsidering if he would let her in.

She looked upset. And her shoulder-length coffee-colored hair was plastered against her head and cheeks. She'd obviously had a run-in with the rain, and she didn't look any more pleased about her encounter with the precipitation than he was.

"What does she want?" Ryan asked Lena.

"She said it was personal. That she *urgently* needed to speak to you."

Of course it was personal. It couldn't be anything but. Old scores to settle and all of that. And the urgent part? Well, that was expected, too. Things always seemed urgent when it came to the Nash family.

This little visit was no doubt about her father. Maybe he'd attempted suicide again. Or maybe Richard Nash had filed yet another frivolous lawsuit to right the wrong that he felt had been done to him. Either way, it couldn't be good.

"She's probably here to try to kill me," Ryan mumbled under his breath.

And it wasn't a joke.

A thought like that should normally have elicited fear or at least a sense of dread, but it'd been a while since he'd felt fear. That could happen when a man had lost everything: the woman he loved and their child.

There was literally nothing left for him to fear.

Or lose.

What he'd dreaded most had already happened.

"Open the gate," Ryan instructed Lena. "Show her in."

At least Delaney Nash would be a distraction from the storm. Sad but true. He preferred to face an irate, possibly homicidal, adversary than deal with the blasted conditioned responses caused by the weather.

"Lena, do a quick background check on Ms. Nash," Ryan added, because, while he didn't mind the distraction, he preferred to be informed. Especially if Ms. Nash had come with murder on her mind. "I haven't kept tabs on her or her father in a while."

"Sure, boss."

Ryan watched as the gates slid open. Delaney Nash wasted no time. Once she had adequate space, she gunned the engine and started the half-mile uphill drive that would bring her to his doorstep.

He winced when she took one of the curves way too fast. Her tires skidded through slick asphalt, and for a second, one horrible gut-tightening second, Ryan thought she might lose control of her vehicle and crash into the massive oaks that lined the road.

She didn't.

No frantic flash of brake lights. She simply slowed down until she finally came to a stop in the covered entryway of the main house.

"Delaney Elizabeth Nash," Lena said through the intercom. One of the servants opened the front door and escorted his visitor inside. "She's twenty-nine, lives in San Antonio. No police record. She owns a day-care center—small but apparently thriving."

Nothing new. Ryan was already aware of those details. "Anything recent on her or her father?"

Ryan gave the security feed another adjustment so he could follow Ms. Nash's little journey through the foyer and onto the wide spiraling stairs that would take her eventually to his office. Unlike other visitors, not once did she stop or even glance at her surroundings. She kept her attention pinned straight ahead. Zombielike.

Or so he thought.

Until Ryan zoomed in on her face. Definitely not zombie material. She was *determined*. Which meant his theory about her being there to kill him might not be so far off the mark.

He glanced at the purse she was practically hugging to her chest. Did she have a gun in there? More importantly, had she come prepared to use it? Maybe something had set her off and brought their old feud back to the surface.

"She had a baby four months ago," Lena continued. "A son named Patrick Thomas Nash."

Interesting. Not just because he'd never thought of her as the motherly type but because the child had the same surname as hers. "So she's not married?"

"No."

"Save any further details for later," Ryan said to Lena when the servant knocked at his office door.

It was showtime.

"Should I monitor this visit?" Lena asked.

Monitor. As in keep a close watch through the security cameras in case Ms. Nash went ballistic. "No. I expect this won't take long."

And in a louder voice, he instructed Ms. Nash to enter.

The door opened. Slowly. And even though there was no eerie creaking sound from the hinges, the room suddenly seemed to take on the ambiance of a horror movie in which the rain and wind battered the glass and a woman, who no doubt hated him enough to kill him, was slowly revealed.

While she stood in the doorway, with the richly stained mahogany framing her, her gaze slid around the room until it landed on him. Only then did she take a step inside. Not a cautious and calculating step, either. She entered with the same determination that she'd had on her trek up the stairs.

He'd been right about the rain doing a real number on her. Her jacket and slim above-the-knee skirt were blotched. There wasn't a dry spot on her hair, and not much left of her makeup. Nothing except a trace of peach-colored lipstick.

And she looked as if she'd been crying.

That sent a weird curl of emotion through him. It was such a foreign feeling, one he hadn't had in a long time, that it took Ryan a moment to identify it. But those tear-reddened, jade-green eyes brought out more than a few protective instincts in his body.

Whoa.

That was a truly stupid reaction.

Because Delaney Nash certainly wasn't feeling protective toward him.

"Did your father send you?" Ryan asked in an effort to change his train of thought.

She blinked, as if shocked by his question. And her shock surprised Ryan, because he'd been almost certain this visit was about Richard Nash.

"This has nothing to do with my father."

She walked closer, her thin, delicate heels clicking like heartbeats on the hardwood floor, and stopped in front of his desk. She took a deep breath and released it slowly. So slowly that it caused her bottom lip to tremble. "I have a favor to ask."

Yet another surprise, and one that had probably cost her an ample amount of Nash pride. She would no doubt rather eat razor blades than come to him for a favor. Or for anything.

"What do you want?" Ryan tried to sound nonchalant but figured he failed. He was anything but nonchalant. This rain-soaked woman, his enemy, had piqued his curiosity.

Among other things.

That trembling bottom lip and her teary eyes were touching places in his heart that he never wanted touched again. Realizing what was happening, Ryan did a detach. He took a mental step back, put on his best corporate sneer and gave her a callous go-ahead prompt with his hand.

She nodded, nodded again and swallowed hard. "I need to see a picture of your son."

Well, that shot the hell out of his corporate sneer and mental step back. He couldn't stay detached after that. Ryan leaned forward. "Excuse me?"

"I went to the library and looked through all the old newspapers." A rain-drop slipped from the ends of her hair and spattered on his desk. She immediately reached down to wipe it away. "But there wasn't a picture of him."

Because Ryan had refused to give one to the papers. He hadn't wanted anyone, especially strangers, to see his infant son. It was a grief, a hurt so deep, that Ryan hadn't wanted to share it.

He still didn't.

"Why?" he asked, aware that the one word encompassed a lot. Not the least of which, he figured it would generate an explanation. Not necessarily a good explanation. Because after all, this was the daughter of a mentally unstable man who'd repeatedly threatened to kill him.

"You won't believe me if I tell you."

"Try," Ryan insisted.

Her fingers were white-knuckled in their grip on her purse. "Could I please just see his picture? I might be able to save us both a lot of time."

Well, the woman certainly knew how to captivate him. And no, it didn't have anything to do with her vulnerability.

All right, maybe it did.

A little.

But it was a problem that he'd soon remedy. Feelings and emotions carried high price tags, and he didn't intend to go there again. *Ever.* And even if he decided to ease up on that rule a bit, he wouldn't have been looking in Delaney Nash's direction.

"Please," she said, her voice and bottom lip trembling again.

Ryan stared at her while he debated it.

And what a debate it was. Why did she want to see a picture of Adam? Why the vague save-us-some-time excuse?

And why the heck was he even considering her bizarre request?

He didn't owe her a damn thing. She and her father had done everything humanly possible to drag his name through the mud. And all because he'd bested Richard Nash in a business deal.

So what.

He'd bested a lot of people, and they hadn't made death threats or tried to sue him. The old analogy of "if you can't stand the heat" came to mind. Richard Nash obviously couldn't, but instead of getting his wimpy butt out of the kitchen, he'd spent the past year and a half trying to get revenge.

Ryan mentally rehashed the past, and while he was at it, he took a few moments to reflect on the woman standing in front of him. And somewhere amid all of that soul-searching, he felt his hand move in the direction of his top right desk drawer.

He didn't look at the object he extracted. He couldn't. It might be acceptable for her to show her vulnerable side, but Ryan didn't intend to reciprocate.

His heart would break all over again if he looked at that picture of his son. And this time, he wasn't sure he'd be able to survive it.

Keeping his attention fastened to her eyes, Ryan handed her the photo encased in the gold-gilded frame. She didn't look at the image, either. She kept her attention on him, shifted her purse beneath her arm and took the picture, her fingers closing around it as if it were made of delicate crystal that might shatter in her hand.

She mumbled something. A prayer, maybe, then looked down at the photo.

Her eyes widened, her breath stopped, and she brought the picture closer. Studying it. Really studying it. Mere inches from her face.

"Oh, God. Oh. God. He's so small," she said, her voice a breathy whisper. Her bottom lip didn't quiver. It began to shake.

She began to shake.

And she adjusted her purse again so that it was in front of her chest.

"Yes." Ryan had to swallow hard before he could continue. Not just because of her extreme reaction, but because he didn't need the image in front of him to visualize his son's face. It was there. Always there. Burned into his memory and his heart. "Adam was born ten weeks premature."

We almost lost him, Ryan nearly added.

It was an automatic addendum he'd used often in those first days after Adam's birth and his stay in the neonatal unit. Those words had proved to be all too prophetic.

Because they *had* lost him.

"When the accident happened," Ryan added. He cleared his throat, but it didn't help. "My son had only been out of the hospital a few days."

And Ryan was suddenly so sorry he'd opened all of this again. Hoping to undo his mistake, he reached out, snatched the picture from her, put it back where it belonged and slammed the drawer.

"All right. Observation time's over. Start talking. Why are you here, Ms. Nash?"

She shook her head in an almost frantic gesture. "It's hard to tell from the picture. You'd think it'd be easy, but it isn't. It isn't easy at all."

Because she looked and sounded on the verge of losing it, and because he wasn't stupid, he stood and grabbed her purse.

She made a sound of surprise, part gasp, part outrage, but Ryan didn't let that stop him. He rifled through the leather bag to see if she'd indeed brought a gun with her.

No gun.

Just the normal things that might be found in a woman's purse. A wallet, keys, comb, pen and some toiletry items. Oh, and a blue pacifier in a clear plastic case.

Hardly the tools of a would be killer.

She grabbed her bag from him and put it back as a shield in front of her. But not before he saw the circular wet splotch around her left breast. Specifically, the blotch centered around the somewhat prominent outline of her nipple. Her focus followed his to see what had captured his attention, and she actually blushed.

"I nurse my son," she said, obviously not comfortable with the topic. "And I'm late for his feeding."

Ryan wasn't exactly comfortable with it either, but there wasn't anything comfortable about this visit. "Then, maybe you should go to your baby instead of being here?"

"The sitter gave him a bottle. I called her on the drive over."

And that brought the conversation to a temporary grinding halt. It took a moment for Ryan to ask what he knew he had to ask. "Why did you react that way to my son's picture?"

She shrugged in a sort of dismissal that didn't change anything. Every muscle in her face was tight and doing battle with each other. "It doesn't matter. Dr. Keyes can't be right."

Ryan took a moment to try to process her mumblings and that name, but there was nothing in his memory to process. "Who the hell is Dr. Keyes?"

"The fertility specialist I used. I can't have a child on my own. I had to use a donor embryo to become pregnant with my son."

"So?" Ryan said, since he had no idea what else to say. This little talk had taken a bad turn somewhere, and he didn't think it would get back on track anytime soon. Still, he wasn't about to send her on her way until he learned what this visit was all about.

"*So,* Dr. Keyes…" She paused, and what little color she had drained from her face. She stared at him. Well, in his direction anyway. Long moments. But Ryan wasn't sure she was seeing him at all. She seemed to be involved in her own private, intense debate that occupied all of her mental energy.

"I have to go," she said.

She whirled around and had made it halfway to the door before Ryan could catch up with her. He stepped in front of her to block her path so she couldn't leave.

"Finish that thought about Dr. Keyes," he insisted.

He saw more of that intense debate, and she must not have cared much for the conclusion she silently drew. "There's no reason to finish it. I'm sorry I bothered you. I'm sorry for everything."

Again, she started for the door. Tried to step around him. But Ryan did some maneuvering of his own until they were face-to-face. Since she was easily five-nine and was wearing heels, they were practically eye-to-eye, as well.

He caught her scent. Not just her rain-soaked clothes, either. *Her scent.* Something rich and female. Like her tears and her trembling lip, it awakened responses inside him that he'd long since buried.

And he intended for them to stay buried, too.

It was a man-woman thing, he assured himself. And it felt more intense than it actually was because he'd gone so long without sex. His thirty-two-year-old body was simply urging him in a direction he had no intention of going.

Ryan pushed her scent and his primal response aside and stared at her. "Talk," he ordered.

"Trust me, you don't want to hear this."

And judging from her adamant tone, he believed her. But that didn't stop him. "Tell me anyway."

She gave a weary sigh, and her head dropped down. "Dr. Keyes thought maybe my donor embryo... Well, he thought it might have been cloned."

"Say what?" Because Ryan had to know what was going on in her eyes, he cupped her chin and lifted it.

He didn't like what he saw.

She was afraid. That fear didn't do much to calm his own suddenly raw nerves.

Her lashes fluttered down, or rather tried to, but she fought it and maintained eye contact with him. "Dr. Keyes believes I might have given birth to a cloned embryo of your son."

Chapter Three

The moment Delaney heard her own words, *a cloned embryo of your son,* she realized what a stupid mistake it'd been to come to Ryan McCall's estate.

Mercy, what had she done?

She'd let the exhaustion, fear and her quest for the truth gnaw away at her, and it had obviously damaged her common sense.

Delaney pulled back her shoulders. She had to get out of there, and she wouldn't wait for her host's permission, either. She stepped around him and started walking.

Ryan McCall reached out, fast, and slammed the door in her face. Not only that, he squeezed himself into the meager space between the door and her, blocking her exit.

"Did you think I wouldn't want an explanation after a bombshell like that?" he challenged.

"That's the problem—I didn't think. And I shouldn't have come," Delaney countered, hoping it would suffice.

It didn't.

When she reached for the doorknob, he snagged her wrist. Alarmed at the physical restraint, she stared at the grip he had on her and then snapped her gaze to his face. She had seen that face a hundred times in the newspapers, and yet he didn't look much like those images that were often plastered in the business section.

Oh, the confidence and the renowned aloofness were there, etched in those glacier-blue eyes. In that almost harshly angled olive-tinged face. Those attributes were even there in his slightly too long but fashionably cut sandy-blond hair. Brad Pitt meets The Terminator. But what the photos had failed to capture were the small things that made him human.

There were tiny lines at the corners of his eyes. Worry lines. And his mouth was tight. Almost rigid. As if it'd been a long time since he'd smiled.

Thinking of Ryan McCall as human,

however, would be yet another mistake, and she'd already made enough of those.

Inside, she was feeling a lot of things. Foolishness for believing this visit would actually alleviate her fears. Anger, mostly directed at herself, for thinking he might have answers. And a sickening dread that all of this could turn even uglier than it already had.

"Explain Dr. Keyes," he pressed. "A cloned embryo of my son. And finally, your *'Dr. Keyes can't be right'* comment."

Delaney stared at him and considered the few options that she had. Clamming up until he backed down was one, but he didn't look like the backing-down type. She studied his eyes.

No. Ryan McCall definitely wouldn't let her walk away from this.

A second option was to sling off his grip and try to muscle her way out of there. She was fairly good in her kickboxing class, but in a physical battle with this man she'd probably lose big-time. Ryan McCall had a good four inches on her and outweighed her by at least fifty pounds. Judging from the fit of his azureblue pullover shirt and black pants, that fifty pounds didn't include much body fat, either.

Of course, her final option was to tell him the truth. There was just one problem with that. She didn't know the truth. Still, he was right. She'd barged into his home. She'd demanded to see a photo of his son, and then she was trying to leave without so much as an explanation. If their situations had been reversed, she'd be blocking his exit exactly the way he was blocking hers.

Figuring she would need it, Delaney drew in a long breath. "Two days ago, a representative from a medical watchdog group called me. He said the New Hope clinic that I used to become pregnant might have done some illegal medical experiments. This group was compiling data so they could request that the Justice Department conduct an investigation."

Judging from his silence, he was considering her words. "Did this representative have any proof of the allegations?"

"If he did, he didn't share it with me. He asked about the procedure I'd had done, and when he mentioned that the clinic might have altered embryos, I talked to Dr. Keyes. Keyes wasn't sure, but he claims a late embryologist might have done some experiments, and that I might have received… Well, you know."

He pondered what she said. "Keyes could be lying."

"He could be." And Delaney would have welcomed the lie. It was far easier than the possible consequences of the truth. "But why would he? Why admit that he has some knowledge about a possible felony?"

His eyes met hers, as had happened several times during the conversation. But for some reason, his scrutinizing regard was even more unnerving than it had been before. It took her a moment to figure out why. They were so close they were practically touching.

Oh.

They *were* touching, she realized.

At least their clothes were. His pants leg was right against her skirt. He was warm. She wasn't. And she felt his warmth all the way through her cool, damp clothes. Since that violated her personal space and then some, she took a huge step back.

The corner of his mouth lifted a fraction. Definitely not a smile. But maybe amusement that she would object to something so small when they had something so large to deal with.

"This Dr. Keyes could be after money," he pointed out.

"You mean some sort of blackmail or extortion? Yes, I considered that, but he made no demands. In fact, he didn't even want to talk to me."

"That still doesn't rule out money."

And the brusque way he said it had Delaney looking beyond their present thread of conversation. "Are we discussing my father now?"

He lifted his right eyebrow just a fraction. "You tell me."

He certainly had a way of riling her. And that particular ability sliced right through all the fear and dread. "Then, no, we're not discussing him."

His eyebrow went even higher. "It wouldn't be the first time he's tried to get money from me."

Delaney really didn't want to go there tonight, but it was obvious that Ryan McCall did. "Look, this isn't about our past. And it's not about my father."

He leaned in. Another personal space violation. "It's *always* about your father."

That was something she couldn't refute. She would forever associate the man standing in front of her with the hostile takeover of her father's manufacturing company. And she'd always associate that with her father's attempted suicide. That was a year and a half ago, and her father had been under psychiatric care ever since. He probably always would be.

But that was just the tip of the iceberg.

There would also be the anger and blame, which her father aimed not only at Ryan McCall but at her, as well. Simply put, her father detested her. He held her partly responsible for his lost business because he felt she hadn't done more to stop it. And she could in turn put the blame for that squarely on Mr. McCall's rather ample shoulders.

McCall stepped to the side, clearing her way to the door. "By the way, I don't believe you."

Good. And her reaction would have probably stayed that way while she made her exit.

If he hadn't continued.

"Just how much money did your father ask you to extort from me?"

Delaney took a step, retraced it and glared at McCall over her shoulder. Part of her knew she should just let it go, but the man had successfully pushed another of her buttons. "Not a cent. And if you think my father would send me here to get anything from you, then you obviously know nothing about either of us."

This time, she actually made it out the door and into the massive hall outside his office.

"Your reaction to my son's picture was a nice touch," he taunted. "The little fluttery breath. The *oh, God.* You must have figured if you could convince me that you had given birth to my son, then I'd hand over everything I own to get him back. The ultimate blackmail scheme. You father would get his revenge, and you'd both be filthy rich. Emphasis on the *filthy.*"

The accusation stung, because there was no way she'd use her son to get back at him. Or anyone. But the wrongful accusation wouldn't stop her from leaving. Delaney hurried toward the stairs.

"Was I supposed to believe that you recognized something in my son's photo?"

he called out. "Or maybe a better question would be—what did you *pretend* to see?"

He was wrong.

That wasn't the better question.

The better question was why had that tiny face seemed familiar? So familiar that it'd made her body respond in the most basic maternal way. She'd felt the slight contraction of her breasts and then the letdown of her milk. A preparation for nursing.

A normal response…as if she'd been looking at the face of her own son.

"HELL," Ryan grumbled.

From the top of the stairs, he watched Delaney Nash race out the front door. Even in heels and a skirt, she was fast. Not exactly the behavior of a lying, scheming woman who had extortion or other unsavory acts on her mind. In fact, it seemed as if his accusations had genuinely upset her.

And that upset him.

Despite his cutthroat reputation and "iceman" moniker that his business cohorts had dubbed him with, he didn't get off by hurting people.

Cursing himself and her visit, Ryan barreled down the stairs after her. He didn't know whether to hope she'd already driven away, or that she was still there.

Fate settled it for him.

She was still there.

Delaney had made it back to her car, which was parked under the portico of the circular driveway. She was definitely trying to leave, but her car wasn't cooperating. With each turn of the key, the engine made a clicking moan. A dead battery maybe.

She tried again. And again. Before she finally smacked her hand, hard, against the steering wheel. Her shoulders slumped, and her head dropped back onto the headrest of the seat. Then she glanced up at the ceiling as if begging for divine assistance.

Ryan walked down the flagstone steps. He knew his movement had drawn her attention because her eyes flew in his direction. For a split second he saw her sheer frustration before she replaced it with a scowl.

He deserved that scowl.

Ryan went to the driver's side of her vehicle, and when she didn't open the door, he reached for the handle. She in turn reached for the lock, but he was slightly quicker than she was. Before she could lock him out, he eased open the door and faced a seriously riled woman.

"You know, most people would have gotten mad and called me a name or two if I'd accused them of attempted extortion," he commented.

Her scowl got worse. "Believe me, I considered a little name-calling."

"It's not too late." He suppressed a wince when lightning zigzagged across the sky. The thunder followed, so loud that it vibrated the roof of the portico. "A lot of people go for jackass, but it's a little overused. How about SOB? It's short and to the point."

She stared at him. "If you're trying to be funny, or charming, you're failing."

"What I'm trying to do..." He had to stop because he had no idea what the heck he was trying to do. Yes, he did owe her a semiapology, but he was going beyond that. He was now somewhere in the uncomfortable realm of attempting to soothe her ruffled feathers.

But she was right.

He was failing.

Huffing, he looked at his household manager, Lena, who was standing in the gaping doorway of the estate. "Have a car brought to the front," Ryan instructed. And because of the storm, he really hated this next part, but after what he'd just put his visitor through, it was something he felt he had to do. "I'll drive Ms. Nash home."

"No, thanks," he heard Delaney say. "I'll call a taxi." Her statement wasn't a suggestion.

Ryan reached across her and placed his hand over hers when she went for the phone nestled between the seats. Not the brightest move he'd ever made. The close confines of the car were, well, close.

Her breath met his.

And Ryan took in more of her than he'd intended. Nothing minty fresh but surprisingly appealing. There it was again. Attraction.

No, wait.

Lust.

He preferred that term. Good old basic lust. It kept things on a purely physical level.

"We're over twenty miles from San Antonio," he explained. "On a country road, no less. It's dark and storming. It'll take a taxi a half hour or more just to get here. I could have you home by then."

He waited for her to debate that.

He also pulled back his hand, and the rest of his body, since being so close really didn't seem like a good idea. Even if it sort of felt right.

Strange.

Why did he have this sudden need to comfort the woman? All she'd done was bring turmoil to his life.

As if he needed more.

Ryan didn't believe her speculation about what had gone on at the fertility clinic. Not that he thought she'd made up the whole thing. No, she was experiencing too much distress for that. The person he doubted was this Dr. Keyes, and before the night was over, Ryan would find out any- and everything he could about the man.

"Well?" Ryan pressed when one of the servants drove a car beneath the portico and parked directly behind Delaney. "You can have a ride, or you can wait. Your choice. My advice is to put aside your resentment and take the ride. That way, you can get home to your son as soon as possible."

That defused the argument he saw in all those shades of green in her eyes, and for the first time since he'd made the offer to take her home, Ryan knew she truly was considering it.

"Thank you," she mumbled.

And then she looked directly at him and repeated the words in a sincere voice.

That impressed him. Why, he didn't know, and Ryan was tired of trying to rationalize his reaction to her. Plain and simple, they just weren't making sense. But then, lust rarely did.

Delaney got out and followed him to the other vehicle. "I'll arrange to have my car towed."

"No hurry." Ryan waited until they were both inside before he continued. "My driver has the night off, but if he can fix it in the morning, I'll have him bring it out to you."

She gave him a considering stare and fastened her seat belt. "Let's get something straight. I appreciate the ride—I really do—but I'd prefer if you didn't try to be nice to me."

Ryan nodded, actually understanding, and he started the car and drove away.

Sheesh.

His heart actually started to race.

"Well, I suppose I could try to accuse you of a few more crimes," he joked. Not because he felt jovial but because his voice partly covered up the sounds of the storm. "That'd keep things from being nice."

She folded her arms over her chest. "I'd prefer no chitchat, either."

Okay. So his diversion had struck out for both of them. "Fair enough. After all, we're not exactly in a chitchat relationship, are we?"

"No," she quickly agreed.

But they were in some sort of relationship. An odd one but a relationship all the same. That strangeness had begun with her impromptu visit and had bumped up a few notches with her reaction to Adam's picture.

"For the record, I don't believe the technology exists for cloning a human embryo," Ryan said. "And even if it did, why would a clinic steal the DNA needed for the embryo? Egos being what they are, I'm sure there would be plenty of volunteers who'd want to replicate themselves."

He waited, going back over his argument and hoping it made sense.

"You're right," she said, sounding relieved. But not totally convinced.

Ryan was on the same page with her.

If, and it was huge *if,* the medical staff wanted to cover up an illegal cloning procedure, they might use whatever DNA they had available. Plus, they might not want to use genetic material that could be traced back to anyone specifically. In other words, it possibly made sense to use a deceased donor.

Hell.

That put a rock-hard knot in his stomach. He couldn't bear the thought that anyone had used his son for medical experiments. It reopened the nightmare all over again. The pain of losing Adam and his wife was suddenly as fresh, as brutal, as it had been that stormy afternoon of the accident.

He tried—and failed—to stop the memories. The slow-motion, dreamlike feel of the call from the hospital. His frantic arrival. Ryan remembered the sterile smell, the look of pity on the ER doctor's face. First, the doctor had pronounced his son dead, and then fifteen minutes later, his wife had lost her own fight for life. The entire time lapse between that first call and those last words was less than an hour.

And in those minutes, Ryan's life had changed forever.

"I'm sorry," he heard Delaney say.

For a second he was afraid he'd voiced his grief aloud and that she was offering him sympathy. He could handle a lot of things, but sympathy wasn't one of them. He preferred her venom to that.

"I shouldn't have come," she continued. So no sympathy. At least none expressed anyway. Merely a further explanation of her visit. "Not without proof, and proof is something I'll never get, because this has all been just a really bad scare."

A really bad scare?

Not exactly his take on things.

A scare maybe for her because, as a parent, she'd no doubt wonder if the hypothetical cloning had done anything to harm her son. However, for Ryan the whole ordeal hadn't been as much of a scare as it had been a huge setback to his healing. For one moment, one too-short moment, he'd considered the possibility that Adam was alive, that he'd been given a second chance.

A chance that was snatched away once reality set in.

Because there were no second chances.

Now, what was left was the aftermath, and Ryan knew that the aftermath was the hard part. In fact, the only thing harder was the question he'd been aching to ask her.

"Does Adam resemble your son?"

He waited.

Held his breath.

And would have prayed if he'd known what to pray for.

It obviously wasn't an easy question for Delaney. She sat there in silence. The only sound was the rhythmic slap of the wipers, the rain and their uneven breathing.

"It's hard to say," she said, choosing her words carefully. "In that picture, your son was so tiny. Mine was born full-term. Eight pounds, seven ounces. He had chubby cheeks. Still does," Delaney added in a whisper.

Full-term. One of the joys of parenthood that Ryan had never gotten to experience. But then, Adam's life had been so short, that neither he nor his son had experienced a lot of things.

While he gave her answer some thought, he tested the high beams of his headlights, but they merely bounced back the reflection of the rain. Ryan switched back to low beams and fastened his attention on the dark, slick road that would take them to the highway.

"You don't happen to have a picture of your son, do you?" Ryan asked.

"No." Her response was as fast as the bolt of lightning that slashed on the horizon in front of them.

She was lying.

And she was really bad at it.

Her voice actually cracked. There was, no doubt, a picture or two tucked inside her wallet. What new mother wouldn't carry around photos of her baby? Still, Ryan had no intentions of calling her on that lie. In a way, he welcomed it. Because if he saw a photo of her son, he'd scrutinize it and pick it apart until he forced himself to see something. *Anything.* That would only cause the hope to grow.

There was no room left in his heart for hope.

"I don't know if my father ever contacts

you," she said. Out of the corner of his eye, Ryan watched her twist the trio of rings she had on her thumb, pinkie and middle fingers of her right hand. The one on her middle finger had a tiny jeweled butterfly charm dangling from it. "But if he does, I'd prefer that you not mention anything about this visit."

"Your father only contacts me through his lawyers. And the last thing I'd discuss with him or anyone else is what happened tonight."

"Thank you." She paused and did more of that nervous fidgeting with her fingers. Delicate fingers. For that matter, a delicate face. Not drop-dead gorgeous, but attractive in a woman-next-door sort of way. Unfortunately, he found that appealing.

Even though that hadn't been the case until tonight.

"But you will check up on Dr. Keyes and the embryologist, won't you?" Delaney asked.

"Absolutely. If there's some kind of scam, I'll find out."

She blew out a long breath, probably not from relief. By now, she was probably kicking herself for even coming to the estate.

He understood how she felt.

There was another flash of lightning, and as the white-hot spear sliced through the darkness, Ryan thought he saw something on the road just ahead. A shadow, maybe. Maybe one of the horses had gotten out of the pasture. He automatically leaned in closer to the windshield, trying to look through the rain and the murky night to determine what it was.

But it was too late.

The dark-colored car came out of the thick curtain of rain. Not on the other side of the road, either.

Right at them.

Ryan heard Delaney scream. A sound of terror that he was sure he would remember for the rest of his life.

If he had a rest of his life, that is.

As he swerved to the right, it occurred to him that this could turn out to be a fatal accident. He knew what was out there.

A deep, six-foot-wide irrigation ditch.

Almost certainly overflowing with rainwater.

A second later, Ryan took out the almost certainly. Even though he tried to keep the car on the road, he wasn't successful. They hit the narrow shoulder of soggy, slick gravel, skidded and then plunged right into the watery ditch.

Chapter Four

One second Delaney was breathing.

Then, she wasn't.

The air bag hit her face and chest. The impact of the collision into the ditch, coupled with that slam, knocked the breath right out of her. Before she could react, she felt the icy cold water begin to gush into the car, spilling onto her feet and legs.

Reality quickly set in.

They were no longer on the road. The car was on its side, her side, harshly angled into a gaping ditch. The collision had crushed in her door, so much so that it vised against her right shoulder.

Trapping her.

If she didn't do something fast, she was going to die.

She forced herself not to panic. No

easy feat. Her heart was already pounding, and adrenaline was pumping through her.

Frantically, Delaney batted back the milky-white air bag so she'd have some room to maneuver and so she could see. Beside her, she felt Ryan do the same. She wasn't successful. With each jab of her fist, each slam of her hands, the air bag shifted, but there was no place for it to go. And along with the crushed-in interior, it was literally holding her in place.

The water didn't cooperate, either. It got deeper. Fast. It came in not as a trickle but a flood. Rushing into the car through the edges of the windows. The doors. And from the floor. Filling it. It rose past her knees. To her waist.

And it just kept on coming.

Along with it came the panic. The fear. She had to get out of there.

She felt Ryan's hand bump against her left hip. Because Delaney was still battling the air bag, she didn't immediately realize what he was doing. She quickly became aware that he was unlatching her seat belt.

"Come on," he said.

It wasn't a shout, but a calmly spoken

statement as if this weren't the life-and-death situation it had quickly become.

Ryan didn't wait for her to comply. He caught on to her shoulder. Pulling. Tugging. Delaney did some maneuvering of her own. She rammed her forearm into the air bag, shoving it aside, and she slipped through the opening and into Ryan's waiting arms.

It wasn't an easy fit.

Even though his side of the car wasn't bashed in, there was an air bag in the way, and he hauled her onto his seat, sandwiching her between the air bag, the steering wheel and his solid body.

He didn't waste any time. With the exception of headlights that were buried beneath the water, it was pitch-dark and she couldn't see much, but Delaney heard the soft grind of his window. It seemed to take an eternity to lower.

With each passing second, her heart beat faster. She prayed, while the water got deeper. Rushing into the car and rising until it swirled around her chest.

Then the soft grinding sound stopped.

The window stopped.

The headlights vanished.

Ryan cursed. Still not with much emotion. The stalled window and lack of light didn't deter him. He slammed his shoulder against his door.

It didn't budge.

Another slam. So hard that it shook the entire car and sent a wave of water careening right into her face. Delaney gasped. Nearly panicked. But then she thought of her son. Of Patrick. If she panicked, she'd die.

Because of him, she had to stay alive.

Somehow.

Delaney pulled in a long breath, holding it in her lungs. It wasn't a moment too soon. The muddy water surged and rose. Racing in all around them, swirling and coiling, smothering, until it covered her throat. Her chin. And finally, her entire face.

God, she couldn't breathe.

Even though there wasn't nearly enough space for her to escape, she scrambled toward the narrow opening of the window, but Ryan held on to her. That didn't do much to steady her heart or ease the overwhelming feeling of terror building inside her.

She lost the battle she'd been fighting with the panic. She had to have air. She had to breathe. She had to get out of there now.

Still, Ryan held on to her.

Why?

She forced herself to think, to calm down so she could conserve what little oxygen she had left in her lungs. It worked. After only a few seconds, it occurred to her what he might be doing. He was probably waiting for the car to be totally immersed so the pressure would be equal on both the inside and outside. Only then could they open the door and get out.

It was their one chance at surviving.

Ryan made another sway of movement. Not a battering motion as before. Delaney did some moving of her own, trying to find the door handle so she could try to open it.

He beat her to it.

Her fingers closed over his. His skin was so cold. Like death. But she pushed the eerie thought aside, and their joined hands pulled back the handle.

The door opened.

Relief rushed through her, but Delaney knew this didn't mean they were out of danger. They still had to make their way out of the ditch.

Ryan hooked his arm around her waist and got them out of the car and into the shadowy water. She pushed her feet against the side of the vehicle and used it as leverage to propel them forward. So did Ryan.

Together, they surfaced.

Delaney gasped, pulling in the much-needed fresh air, and she reached for anything she could use to haul herself out of the ditch. She managed to latch on to a handful of mud and grass. Unfortunately, the soft squishy mixture wasn't good grasping material. It slipped right through her fingers, and she would probably have sunk right back into the water if it hadn't been for Ryan.

He stabbed his elbow into the muddy embankment, using it to anchor them, and in the same motion, he thrust them both forward. Away from the water and the car. And onto the gravel shoulder.

To safety.

Her lungs felt starved for air, and Delaney sucked in several feverish breaths. Beside her, she heard Ryan do the same.

But other than that, he didn't take any more time to recover from the ordeal.

Scrambling to get to his knees, Ryan tried to position himself in front of her. But he couldn't. It took Delaney a moment to realize why. Their hands were locked together. Specifically, their fingers. She felt around and located the problem. The butterfly charm on her ring had somehow slipped beneath Ryan's wedding band.

He pulled his hand away, still trying to reposition himself. Delaney did the same. A few tugs, and she felt something snap. The butterfly charm broke off, and Ryan and she were free.

Ryan immediately placed himself between her and the country road. Even through the rain and darkness, Delaney could see that he was searching for something. His eyes whipped first to one end of the road and then to the other.

Delaney did the same, but she saw nothing other than the night and the rain. Even the momentary illumination from a flash of lightning didn't reveal anything. Definitely no sign of the other car that had careered toward them.

The car that had caused the accident.

Ryan cursed again, and this time, there was raw, uncut emotion.

Delaney wasn't immune to emotion either as a sickening feeling coursed through her.

Perhaps this had not been an accident at all.

"I'LL BE RIGHT BACK with your statements," Sheriff Dillon Knight informed Ryan. The lanky, denim-clad sheriff stood and headed for the exit of the interview room. "You and Ms. Nash can leave as soon as you've signed everything."

Ryan glanced at Delaney, who was across the room on the phone talking to her babysitter. She nodded, an acknowledgment that she'd heard the sheriff.

Acknowledgement and relief.

Relief was certainly a reasonable reaction considering they'd been at the Grandville hospital and then the sheriff's office for two-and-a-half hours. During that time, they'd been questioned, examined by one of the local doctors, bandaged, and then questioned again. What they hadn't had was a moment of privacy or peace. Delaney probably wanted nothing more than to get out of there and go home to her son. Ryan overheard snippets of her conversation with her babysitter to confirm that.

Are you sure Patrick's all right?

Please tell him I'll be there soon.

Tell him I love him.

Kiss him good-night for me.

Definitely the words of a mother worried about her child, even if her child was probably too young to know what those reassurances meant.

They'd been lucky. Damn lucky. They'd gotten away with a bruise on Delaney's right arm, a scrape on his neck and some assorted nicks. They would no doubt be stiff and sore for a few days, but all in all, the injuries were minor.

Lucky indeed.

Ryan took a long sip of the sludge-black coffee that the sheriff's deputy had provided. The too-strong brew was bitter, obviously hours past its prime, if it'd ever had a prime. And yet Ryan welcomed the heat. Plus, it gave his hands something to latch on to so that he wouldn't fidget. It was either that or stuffing his hands in his pockets. The coffee won out in the end. Too bad it couldn't stop his mind from fidgeting, but that was asking a lot of mere hot coffee.

Even though he was in dry clothes—loaner jeans and a T-shirt courtesy of the hospital—the icy coldness of the water had seemed to seep all the way into his bones. It was a cold he'd never forget.

And he wasn't about to forget the *accident* anytime soon, either.

As he'd already done a dozen times, Ryan went through the events that led up to them being plunged into the irrigation ditch. To paraphrase an old saying, the devil was in the details, and his gut feeling was that something sinister had happened tonight.

The road leading to the estate was private. Hardly used by anyone but his staff and him. Yet, the other car had been there. At the sharpest curve of the road near the deepest, widest part of the irrigation system. With no headlights on. And on the wrong side of the road. It'd come right at them.

Then disappeared.

Ryan didn't think it was a phantom or a ghost car. Nor was it some illusion caused by the storm.

No.

The vehicle had been real. And now the question was to find out who'd been behind the wheel, why they had been on the road, and why the driver had done what he or she had done.

Ryan would get answers to those questions, and he wouldn't rely only on the sheriff to help him. He'd call Quentin Kincade, his security guru, and get some investigators on this immediately.

"We won't have to be here much longer," he heard Delaney say. Ryan wasn't sure if she was trying to convince herself or him. She hung up the phone, scrubbed her hands over her arms and started to pace.

Yep. She was a pacer.

Ryan had learned that about her over the past two-and-a-half hours. A pacer, a lip nibbler and a mumbler. He'd also discovered that she wasn't a coffee drinker, had instead opted for bottled water. Perhaps because she was nursing and didn't want the caffeine, or maybe because she was already too jittery.

"Are you okay?" he asked.

"Sure." She'd answered too quickly for it to be anything but rote. It did stop her, however. She quit pacing, briefly met his eyes and shook her head. The motion sent a lock of her now-dry dark brown hair slipping down onto her forehead. She raked it away. "I just need to get out of here."

Ryan understood completely. The fatigue was quickly becoming a factor, and he wasn't sure he could think straight much longer. As a rule, he never liked to be in a situation where he didn't have a clear head. "If the sheriff's not back in a few minutes, I'll see what I can do to speed things up."

Another nod. "Thank you." She paused a heartbeat. "For everything."

"You're welcome."

Because it'd been a while, too long, since he'd said something that genuinely cordial to anyone, Ryan decided it was a good time to shut up and drink his god-awful coffee. This forced proximity, and the remnants of the danger had created some kind of weird intimacy between Delaney and him.

Intimacy that neither of them wanted.

She folded her arms over her chest and resumed her pacing in her borrowed jeans and the faded blue T-shirt that swallowed her. It was at least three sizes too big, and yet it somehow managed to skim and accent every curve of her body. And she had some curves.

Something he was sorry he'd noticed.

Worse, he hadn't noticed it just once. His attention kept going back to her—her body, her face, those eyes—and Ryan just kept forcing his attention on something else. Anything else.

Their respective coping behaviors, the pacing, the coffee drinking, the diverted attention worked for several moments. Until the silence settled a little too uncomfortably around them.

"Nothing like this has ever happened to me before," Delaney said. "Not even a fender bender. For a couple of moments there, I thought we were going to die."

He'd thought the same thing, but Ryan kept it to himself.

"Do you think this is connected to what Dr. Keyes told me?" she asked.

It was the billon-dollar question, and it was a possible connection they hadn't withheld from the sheriff.

Well, in a way, they hadn't.

Delaney had been careful not to accuse

the doctor outright of a crime, but she had told Sheriff Knight about the unsettling call from the medical watchdog group. What she'd left out, however, was any mention of cloning. It was as if she were trying to strike that particular detail from her mind. Ryan was willing to bet she hadn't been any more successful at it than he'd been.

However, the cloning allegation wasn't the only factor to be considered here.

"I've made enemies," Ryan admitted, staring down into his coffee. And that was a massive understatement. "This could have happened because of me."

Not an easy admission to make to her, and Ryan hoped—no, he prayed—that this deed wasn't on his head. He already had enough unresolved issues in his life without adding this latest episode involving Delaney Nash.

She came to a halt directly in front of the gray metal table where he was sitting and waited until their eyes met. "You didn't mention anyone specific to the sheriff."

He lifted a shoulder. "Because there's a lot more than just one. But then, I don't have to remind you of that."

Delaney paused a moment and nodded. "No."

She stood there, looking exhausted but determined to dig until they learned the truth. She also looked vulnerable. The vulnerable part wasn't so obvious, but he knew it was just beneath the surface. The fact she was trying to hide it brought out some of his own feelings.

He wanted to protect her.

Which made him an idiot.

Delaney wasn't some money-hungry opportunist out to extort from him. During the past couple of hours, he'd gotten past those particular allegations. But she was his enemy's daughter. And she was embroiled in some kind of…whatever. He couldn't dismiss the potential issues that had surfaced from the New Hope clinic and Dr. Keyes.

Nor would it be wise to overlook the obvious.

"I know we've been through this, but I need you to think hard. Is it possible that your father knew you were coming to see me tonight?" Ryan asked.

He braced himself for her to unleash a vehement protest, A declaration of her father's innocence. After all, it was practically an accusation. A really serious one. Her father's involvement would mean that he'd essentially tried to murder them.

"I didn't tell him," Delaney answered. No protest, and she didn't add anything else for several seconds. "But I suppose he could have found out. I mean, my sitter knew where I was. If he called her, she might have told him."

She became more ashen with each word, and her breath was no longer level. Delaney glanced at the clock on the wall and then motioned toward the door. "I have to go to the ladies' room." She obviously needed to come to terms with what she'd just realized—her father could have been the one behind the wheel of the other car.

"This is a small town and an equally small sheriff's office, so it's my guess that Dillon Knight won't be able to offer you any protection," Ryan added before she could walk away. "If you decide you want or need it, that is." He took a sheet from the notepad that the deputy had left on the table, and he wrote down the phone number of the person who was in charge of his security. "Quentin Kincade. He's a good man. Just call him if you have any concerns. Or if you prefer—you can call me."

Her fingers brushed against his when she took the sheet of notepaper from him. It barely qualified as a touch.

Barely.

But she focused on their hands. Specifically, that touch. She drew her brows together, clutched the paper and retreated.

Ryan took a similar mental step back. Whoa. It was a lot of reaction for a simple touch. A leftover effect from spent adrenaline maybe?

Yes.

That had to be it.

He wasn't about to entertain any other possibility.

He glanced at the ring on her middle finger. "Your butterfly's gone," he said.

"Yes." She glanced at it and nodded. Her forehead bunched up. "It broke off and must have fallen off in the water."

"Was it valuable?"

Another nod. "To me it was."

Yet another feeling he didn't want. Sheesh. Why did he have a sudden urge to head back to the ditch and try to find the butterfly?

He was obviously losing it, that's why.

"I really am sorry for everything that's happened," she said.

There was a slight hitch in her voice. An edgy nervousness that hadn't been there before that whole touching encounter or the butterfly conversation. Ryan didn't know which had caused the change, and he didn't want to know.

"I'm sorry, not just for tonight, but also for what went on with my father."

She didn't give him time to respond. Not that he would have known what to say to her apology anyway. Delaney turned and headed for the door, leaving him alone in the quiet room to ponder what the hell had just happened.

He looked down at his fingers, at the spot where they'd made contact. A spot just above his wedding ring that was still tingling. Potent stuff. Like his entire encounter with her.

The hypothetical cloning.

Her emotional reaction to his son's photos.

Their argument.

The accusations.

The car accident.

All of it, every excruciating detail, was whirling around in his head until it was quickly becoming a blur. Still, Ryan forced himself to concentrate, to focus on one facet of the problem at a time. And one facet was definitely Delaney. Not her situation. But Delaney herself. His body wanted her, no sense denying that, but what he wanted more was answers about what was going on.

Was the technology for cloning still in the hypothetical stage? Had the New Hope clinic done the unthinkable? Or better yet, had they attempted it, failed, but for some reason wanted to let Delaney think they had succeeded?

While that theory made his heart ache for the son he'd never see again, it was a theory that had merit. And that brought him back to square one. Because that theory would no doubt involve some means of trying to get him to pay up for what was probably a hoax.

In this case, Ryan had to wonder if that would lead them directly to Richard Nash, Delaney's father.

The door opened, and Ryan braced himself to face Delaney again, but he relaxed when he saw Sheriff Knight with a piece of paper in his hand.

"I need you to sign at the bottom," Knight instructed. "And then you're free to go. By the way, your driver's waiting for you out front."

Ryan complied, using the pen from the desk, and he handed the signed statement to the sheriff. "I'll be hearing from you?"

The man nodded. "As soon as I've had a chance to conduct a thorough investigation."

Thorough, perhaps, but it was an exercise that might not yield a thing. Ryan hadn't remembered hearing the sound of the other car hitting its brakes, and there had been no collision between the two vehicles. And that meant, there probably wouldn't be any physical evidence.

"Go home," Sheriff Knight added, as if reading his mind. "Get some rest. Let me do my job."

The sheriff was nearly out the door before Ryan stopped him. "But what about Ms. Nash? She's in the ladies' room—"

"She left."

Ryan frowned. "Left?"

"Yeah. Right before I came in here. I

saw her in the hall, had her sign her statement, and asked one of my deputies to drive her home. She said she needed to get back to her little boy."

Along with his tingling fingers, Ryan experienced other sensations he didn't welcome.

Disappointment.

And concern.

Because if the accident hadn't really been an accident, if someone had intentionally set out to harm them tonight, then that meant Delaney, and her son, might still be in grave danger.

Chapter Five

Delaney huffed. Here, it'd been two days since the car crash, and she was still reliving it. Every excruciating, terrifying moment. This had to stop.

Forcing herself to concentrate, she added several notes to the lesson plans for the three-year-old group at her day-care center. And then she reread what she'd just typed.

The notes didn't make sense.

Her mind just wasn't on veggie alphabet activities, bunny sugar cookies and watercolor rainbows. Ironic, since those were usually the kinds of preschool activities that would get her mind off her adult problems.

She tried again, going through the steps of each activity. Calculating a supply list and time allocation. Imagining how the children would react. There'd be smiles, laughter, the excitement of experiencing something new.

But even that couldn't pull her out of her gloomy mood.

Frustrated, she minimized the computer file, got up from her desk, tucked in the corner of her family room, and went to the doorway of the nursery to check on Patrick.

He was still asleep.

Thankfully, the turmoil she'd been experiencing hadn't spilled over to her son. She intended for it to stay that way. Even if there were times, like now, when it seemed an impossible task.

The accident near Ryan's estate was just one of her problems. Even though it was monumental, *and it was,* that wasn't what was troubling her most. No, her top worry stemmed from the whole cloning allegation.

And the fact that perhaps it wasn't an allegation at all.

By now, Ryan had certainly considered that. Probably more than considered it. He was perhaps already conducting his own investigation, and sooner or later that query would encompass finding the truth about Patrick's biological parents.

Biological parents that might include Ryan himself.

At the disturbing thought, Delaney sank onto the sofa and hugged a throw pillow to her chest, hoping to tamp down the emotions that were so close to springing to the surface. Because if what Keyes had seen in the embryologist's records was true, if Patrick was indeed a clone of Ryan's son, then...

"Ryan might have a claim to get custody of my son," Delaney whispered.

There.

She'd said it.

And even more, it was true. Too bad she hadn't realized that *before* she made the frantic drive out to see Ryan. What she should have done was taken the time to examine the consequences of that visit. Mercy, she'd all but handed him the very information he could use against her.

Simply put, if Ryan could prove that he was Patrick's biological father, he could try to take her son from her.

And Ryan had the money and resources to do it.

Delaney forced herself to stay calm, but inside she was screaming. She couldn't lose her child. She just couldn't. Patrick was everything to her.

Her son.

Her life.

Delaney had dreamed of him long before she'd ever stepped foot in the New Hope clinic. Even before she'd gotten pregnant with him, she had believed that one day she would have her own family.

And she'd succeeded.

Despite her infertility and the fact that after several miserable failed relationships, she had given up on finding a significant other, she'd had faith that one day she would have a baby. Now, Ryan could snatch that all away from her.

At least, he could try.

She couldn't let him succeed.

The sound of the phone ringing shot through the room. She'd been so deep in thought, it took her a moment to realize what it was. One glance at caller ID, and she knew this was a call she needed to take.

"Sheriff Knight," Delaney greeted. She got up from the sofa and closed the nursery door so the conversation wouldn't wake Patrick. "I've been waiting to hear from you. Did you find out anything?"

"I did an investigation, even called in one of the Rangers to assist me, but I couldn't find anything to indicate this was more than just an accident."

"An accident?" She knew her tone conveyed her doubts.

The sheriff didn't reconfirm it immediately. Instead, he paused and obviously went for a little rewording. "There's no evidence it was foul play."

No.

But that didn't mean it wasn't.

There were some serious shades of gray here, and Delaney had given those shades a lot of consideration in the two days since she and Ryan McCall had gone into the irrigation ditch. The incident could have been some kind of warning. Maybe meant for Ryan. Or her. Neither of them could be excluded as the primary target.

I've made enemies, Ryan had admitted to her that night at the sheriff's office.

Not exactly late-breaking news. On his rise to being one of the most successful businessmen in the state, he'd no doubt made dozens of enemies. Including her father. And if that was the particular enemy who'd been in the other car, then maybe both she and Ryan had been his targets.

That thought made her feel sick to her stomach.

Yes, her father had been toeing the line between sanity and mental instability for a year and a half, but Delaney had a difficult time believing he would try to kill her.

"What about Dr. Keyes at the New Hope clinic?" Delaney asked the sheriff. "Were you able to question him?"

"He's on vacation and can't be reached." Judging from his tightly spoken explanation, Knight wasn't pleased that he hadn't been able to interrogate the man. "But I'll definitely interview him when he returns."

"*If* he returns," she corrected.

"You know something I don't?" he quickly countered.

"No. But if Dr. Keyes believes he's under investigation for illegal medical practices, he might not be so eager to get back to work."

"True. That's why I went ahead and called the clinic director, Dr. Emmett Montgomery, while you were writing your account of what happened. Montgomery knew all about the watchdog group's concerns and the alleged records of the embryologist, William Spears, and Montgomery dismissed them."

She was taken aback at the disclosure. "So he told you about the cloning allegation?" Not that Delaney had thought it wouldn't surface at some point.

"He did, and he said the Physicians Against Unethical Practices group makes a lot of unfounded allegations. Montgomery insists he runs a clean clinic, and that Spears wouldn't have been allowed to do any kind of illegal experiments at New Hope."

"And you believe him?"

"Unless I find something to the contrary, I do. But if anything comes up, I'll give you a call."

Delaney considered several responses, including a good airing of her concerns about her father, but she settled for a polite thank-you and goodbye.

She clicked off the phone and barely had time to put it back on the coffee table when there was a knock at the door. Normally, an unexpected visitor wouldn't have sent her heart pounding, but since the accident, her heart rate and her life had felt out of control.

Trying not to make a sound, Delaney tiptoed to the door and peeked out the corner of one of the stained-glass sidelight windows. The rippled water-glass didn't obscure the person standing on her front porch. One glimpse at her visitor, and her heart beat even harder.

"We need to talk," Ryan called out, seeming to know she was there. She realized there were windows on her garage doors, and if he'd looked inside, he would have easily seen her car. A car that Ryan would recognize. After all, she'd driven it to his estate, and in turn, his driver had repaired and delivered it to her house.

Delaney considered walking away from the door, going into the nursery and hiding. That's what she desperately wanted to do anyway. That, and to hold on to her son. But hiding would only delay the inevitable. One way or another, she had to face Ryan and convince him that no matter what the cloning allegations proved or disproved, her son's custody was not up for negotiation.

DNA might be a biological indicator, but it damn sure didn't make a person a parent.

She was Patrick's parent. His *only* parent.

Delaney jerked open the door as if she'd declared war on it, but the brief fit of temper faded when she saw Ryan. He looked as if he hadn't slept in the two days since she'd last seen him.

And maybe he hadn't.

She certainly hadn't gotten much sleep.

Even with the fatigue, he still had an air of ruthlessness and authority about him. And good fashion sense. Perfectly tailored khakis, a classy black jacket, and a bronze-colored pullover shirt that was almost the same color as his hair. Obviously this was his *GQ* casual look, and it made her wonder if he even owned a pair of scruffy jeans. Probably not. He looked expensive. Smelled expensive.

And was.

"May I come in?" he asked.

Delaney hesitated, dreading the inevitable, but she finally stepped aside so he could enter. He walked in hesitantly. And he made a sweeping glance around the room before his eyes came to hers. There was no obvious disapproval in his expression for her modest lifestyle. But she had to wonder what he thought of the way she lived. His bedroom was probably larger than her entire house.

"Sheriff Knight called me about a half hour ago," Ryan commented.

She nodded. "I just got off the phone with him. He believes what happened was an accident."

Ryan made a sound that could have meant anything. Or nothing. In fact, the sound was his only response, and it further unnerved her.

She opened her mouth to ask why he was there, but he spoke before she could. "I went back to the irrigation ditch, but I didn't find the butterfly you lost from your ring."

Okay. That threw her a little off. "You actually looked for it?"

"Not specifically." He slid his hands into his pockets. "But I kept my eye open for it. You said it was valuable."

"Yes. Well, valuable in a sentimental way." And even though she hadn't intended to give him an explanation, for some reason she felt as if she owed him one.

Good grief.

He'd actually looked for a tiny citrine

butterfly that was smaller than a raisin? In a massive irrigation ditch, no less.

"I bought the charm the day I found out I was pregnant with Patrick. A celebration gift of sorts. You know, the whole cocoon to the butterfly transformation thing?"

Sweet heaven, she was babbling. Worse, she was going on about something he couldn't possibly understand, much less care about.

"I know," he said, just as she was ready to move to another subject. *Any* subject. "I bought myself something when I reached my first business milestone."

"What you'd buy—a third-world country?" Yes, it was petty and smart-ass, but Delaney couldn't help it. Besides, for one brief second, the banter eased some of the unbearable tension between them.

"No. The third-world country came later." No smile. But the remark was enough to let her know that he, too, could play sm   ally, I bought an antique p   at had once belonged to a Defender of the Alamo." He shrugged. "A shrink would probably say I was trying to give myself a meaningful personal history to counteract my actual personal history, which wasn't so meaningful."

Delaney didn't want to be fascinated by that, but she was. "Was that what you were trying to do?"

A muscle flicked in his jaw. "Of course."

He left it at that. Which was just as well. She'd heard rumors that as a child Ryan had been abandoned by his teenaged mother, passed from one family member to another and then channeled into the foster-care system. He never mentioned these childhood events in interviews. And it probably wasn't a good thing to discuss with him now. Delaney didn't want to feel any sympathy for this self-made man.

"Why are you here?" she asked.

He waited a few more seconds. There were several flicks of his jaw muscles and a slight shift of his posture. "I've been thinking about what happened the other night. In fact, I've given a lot of thought to everything that's gone on since you walked into my office. You know where this is leading, where it has to lead, right?"

That question did away with the semi-kindheartedness she felt over his butterfly search and his less-than-perfect childhood.

"That depends on perspective, and from my perspective, all of it ends here. The accident was just that—an accident. And the allegations by the medical watchdog group are merely allegations."

"You really believe that?"

She stared at him. "I *have* to believe that."

"Well, I can't take the head-in-the-sand approach. For one thing, it could be dangerous."

Delaney wanted to dash off a cool comeback, but his warning put a sizable dent in her composure. "You're working under the assumption that what happened is connected to the rumors associated with the New Hope clinic."

"No. I'm working under the assumption that the attempted murder, aka the car accident, was connected to one of us. That means, it could ultimately be connected to your son."

She shook her head and began to twist one of her rings. "But you said you didn't believe the technology exists for human cloning."

"I don't. But someone else might believe it. Someone associated with the clinic who wants the watchdog group's allegations to go away."

"Are you saying—"

"I'm saying we need answers, and I don't think we can rely on Sheriff Knight to get them for us."

The ring fidgeting wasn't helping, so she tried pacing. Not far, and she kept herself positioned between Ryan and the nursery. "And how do you propose we get answers?"

He reached into his inside jacket pocket and extracted a small, clear plastic bag. Inside was what appeared to be a Q-tip.

"It's a buccal swab test kit to collect genetic material," Ryan explained.

Oh, God.

Delaney's pulse was suddenly thick and throbbing and vibrating throughout her entire body. She actually dropped back a step to put some distance between herself and the test kit.

"It's not invasive, definitely not painful," Ryan went on. He paused and cleared his throat. "According to the doctor, all you have to do is swab the inside of your son's mouth."

And then what?

The question exploded inside her head, but the words never made it past the tight clamp in her throat.

"We can have Patrick's DNA tested," Ryan continued a moment later. Not easily. He was obviously having his own personal problems with speech. His voice was strained and clipped. "Then, we'll know."

Yes.

Then, they'd know.

And that's what terrified Delaney.

Because she wasn't sure she could live with the answer.

Chapter Six

Ryan hadn't even been aware that he was holding his breath until he became light-headed. Actually, he began to get down-right dizzy. Since collapsing would put a serious dent in the stalwart, rock-hard image he wanted to portray, he drew in a long breath.

And he waited.

Simply put, it was entirely possible that Delaney held his future—and his heart—in her hands.

He could probably force her to have the test done. *Probably.* Getting a court order would be time-consuming and tricky, but he could use his team of highly paid law-yers to cut through the layers of red tape. But the lawyers and a court order would no doubt end the semiamicable bonds that

Delaney and he had forged while fighting their way out of the irrigation ditch.

At least, Ryan hoped there were bonds, because he needed something, anything, to gain her cooperation. And her trust.

He didn't want to wait weeks for a court order and weeks beyond that for her to comply. Even if all of this was a long shot. And it *was* a long shot, Ryan reminded himself—again. Too bad his heart had latched on to that remote possibility and wouldn't let go.

He had to know if Patrick Nash was his son.

"I need to sit down," Delaney said, a second before she dropped down into a bulky armchair in the living room.

The chair had a cheery floral pattern with various shades of blue and green. For that matter, everything he could see about the house was cheery, even though the single-story residence was modest by anyone's standards.

"I thought about calling you first," Ryan said. He followed her and sat on the sofa directly across from her. The only thing that separated them was a coffee table covered not with knickknacks and magazines but with a pale blue blanket, a floppy-looking teddy bear and a pair of baby's socks made to look like running shoes. "Maybe then the DNA request wouldn't be such a shock."

"It would have still been a shock," Delaney quickly let him know.

She was right. This was not a blow he could have softened with a phone call or with chitchat about her lost ring and his antique pocket watch. Besides, if he'd alerted her to what he wanted, she might have grabbed Patrick and gone on the run.

He couldn't risk that.

"We have to know," Ryan added, praying she'd agree. Unfortunately, her curiosity was probably overshadowed by her fear of where all of this might lead.

"Do we?" But Delaney immediately waved away her own question because she knew the answer. What she couldn't wave off was the pain all of this was causing her.

Ryan understood that.

Even now, nearly forty-eight hours after her visit to the estate, he was still debating if he should ask her to submit her son to the DNA test he'd brought with him. But, heaven help him, he didn't see another way around the problem of not knowing.

Delaney closed her eyes, lowered her head and tucked her feet beneath her. Practically a fetal position. She didn't even attempt polite conversation, which was just as well. They were past that stage.

Ryan sat there, waiting and watching her as she went through her own personal version of hell. In fact, he couldn't take his eyes off her.

Like the night of her visit, she didn't have on a business suit. She was barefoot. Her toes were painted flamingo pink. She wore denim shorts that revealed a nice pair of shapely legs and a snug little stretchy top the color of a ripe mango. It outlined her breasts.

Of course, he shouldn't have even noticed that.

Ryan leaned in closer and fought the urge to reach for her—not because of the sexual energy sizzling between them but because he desperately wanted to comfort her.

An impossible task.

Especially coming from him.

That didn't stop his hand from moving

closer, reaching out, until he slid his fingers over hers.

Her eyelids flew up. She was obviously startled. Her accusing gaze slashed to his. Ryan didn't move back. He kept his hand in place. Probably the wrong place since he was touching her. But he kept it there anyway.

"I'm sorry," he said.

"Are you?" But before he could respond, Delaney dismissed it by shaking her head. She also moved her hand. And his. Inching back away from him.

Recoiling.

Before the recoil was complete, Ryan caught a whiff of baby powder. And her. Something distinctly female. Somehow, it was the unique scent that cut through everything and made its way to his nose.

Ryan reminded his nose not to get any bad ideas to pass on to the rest of his body.

He forced his attention away from her and looked around the simply furnished room. Better to concentrate on the decor than gawk at her. It was clean, uncluttered and efficient. A lot like the woman who owned it. What was missing was the baby.

But there were two rooms just off to his left. One of them was probably the nursery.

The *nursery*.

For such a simple word, it caused a flurry of emotions.

"What would you do with the DNA results?" Delaney challenged.

Talk about a loaded question, and he was positive she wouldn't care for his response. "I think we should get the results first, and then we can discuss it."

Nope. Judging from her scalpel-sharp glare, she didn't like what he had to say. "We'll discuss it now."

"Fair enough." And it was what he'd expected. Ryan had assumed it would take an argument, or even several of them, to convince her. "I figure there's only a slim chance that you received a cloned embryo. And if you did, there's an even slimmer chance that the embryo was created from genetic material taken from my son, Adam. So look at it this way—the test results could give you peace of mind."

She made a sound. A short burst of air. Almost a laugh, but it was laced with irony. "I've pretty much given up on that whole peace-of-mind thing." Her glare softened then faded. And she bunched up her forehead. "I'm trying really hard not to be terrified of you, but I'm failing."

Her honesty broke down his defenses in a way that nothing else could have. Not good. He couldn't allow that. Ryan was positive he would need those defenses before this was over. "My reputation—"

"I didn't mean your reputation. I'm talking about Patrick." She moistened her lips and took in a quick breath. "I'm sick over the possibility of losing him to you."

That did it. Many people had called him a cold, heartless bastard, but he would have truly had to be one not to reach out to her. Ryan came off the sofa and maneuvered himself between the coffee table and her chair. Not touching her, exactly, but close enough that if she needed a shoulder to cry on, he'd offer his.

Despite what it would end up costing them both if she accepted.

"I've tried to put myself in your place," she said, her voice quivery now. "And I know I'd be requesting a DNA test—"

"And if I were you, I'd be fighting it."

She lifted her eyes to meet his and gave an uncertain nod, as if she hadn't expected him to understand. "But fighting it won't make this go away, will it? The question of Patrick's paternity is there now, and I don't think you'll stop until you know the truth."

Ryan hoped his silence conveyed that she was right about that. "You need the truth, too, Delaney. Even if it's so you'll have a medical history of your son's biological parents." Because it seemed like a festering wound between them, he slipped the DNA kit back into his jacket pocket. "Did the clinic tell you anything about the couple who supposedly donated the embryo you used?"

"Just the basics. Hair color, eye color, nothing in their backgrounds to indicate there'd be future medical problems." She paused and pursed her lips. "Hair color," she repeated.

He didn't care much for the return of the panicky look in her eyes. "What about it?"

"The donors were both brunettes. Patrick isn't."

Ryan would have definitely pushed for more info, and for her conclusion as to what that meant, if he hadn't been interrupted. The two sounds happened within seconds of each other. His phone rang, and the baby started to cry.

Delaney actually looked relieved and leaped from the chair. "I'll be back," she mumbled, as she disappeared into one of the other rooms.

Ryan stood, trying to get a glimpse of Patrick, but she pulled the door partly shut behind her. He answered his phone while he walked closer.

"What is it, Quentin?" he asked, knowing that his security manager was the only person who'd be calling him during this visit. Ryan peered into the nursery and saw Delaney leaning over the crib to change Patrick's diaper. The baby stopped crying and began to make cooing noises.

The room was decorated in a superhero motif. Plenty of color with various cartoon crusaders in motion. Some on the ceiling directly over the crib. Others, on the walls.

There weren't a lot of toys, but the ones that were in the room were placed strategically around the bed so that Patrick would easily be able to see them. Delaney had obviously put her day-care experience to good use in decorating the baby's room.

"I did deeper background checks on those doctors from New Hope clinic,"

Quentin informed Ryan. "Including the late embryologist, William Spears."

"Go on." Ryan kept his voice low so he wouldn't alert Delaney.

"Spears died of a stroke. A little odd since he was only forty-eight, but he did have a family history of cardiovascular problems. I did some digging, read the medical examiner's report. No sign of foul play."

Well, that was one theory down—that Spears had been murdered to silence him and his alleged illegal research project. "What about Spears's records, the ones that supposedly mentioned the cloning?"

"A lab technician claims to have seen them."

"You mean there's an actual witness?" Ryan tried to remain skeptical and objective. But his heart didn't want that. It wanted proof that Patrick was his son.

"I tracked down the guy, Noel Kendall, but he wouldn't talk to me face-to-face. Had to settle for a phone conversation. He's scared, boss, and it doesn't seem like he's faking it."

"How is he connected to Spears?" Ryan asked.

"Noel Kendall is the one who found Spears dead at the clinic, and according to him, Spears had the hard copy of records in his hands. Noel claims he skimmed through them while waiting for the ambulance to arrive, and then when the records went missing, he got concerned and tipped off the watchdog group. I'm working on getting access to the computer that Spears used. If he left something on it, I'll find it."

It sounded like a long shot, but thankfully Spears wasn't their only source of information. "What about Bryson Keyes and Emmett Montgomery?"

"Neither have criminal records, but seven years ago Keyes was involved in some stem-cell research that was shut down. Not quite illegal at the time, but it fell into the unethical category. He's been squeaky clean ever since."

"I detect a *but* in there," Ryan commented.

"There is. The New Hope clinic has only been at its present location for nineteen months. Prior to that, it was part of Alamo Heights hospital."

Ryan's grip tightened on his phone. Alamo Heights hospital. The place where his wife and son had died. Hell. "Keyes, Spears and Montgomery were working that day?"

"I don't know yet. I'm waiting on phone records. That should tell us something."

Ryan watched as Delaney reached down and scooped the baby into her arms. She murmured something to him, words with a soft, rhythmic cadence that seemed to soothe Patrick. Ryan tried to latch on to some of those soothing effects, because heaven help him, he needed something to settle him down.

"Keep me informed," Ryan told Quentin. He clicked off the phone in the middle of Quentin's goodbye and slipped it back into his pocket.

Delaney's maternal murmurings didn't soothe the baby for long. He started to fuss and crammed his fist into his mouth. She looked over her shoulder at him, as if she'd known all along he was watching her.

"He's hungry. And impatient. Sorry, but he gets priority over our conversation. Baby formula upsets his stomach, and I didn't use the breast pump today, so I can't give him a bottle."

That meant she had to nurse him. Ryan

turned back toward the living room, but not before he saw her sit in the rocking chair next to the crib. She lifted her top.

Damn.

He felt like the worst kind of pervert, but it took every ounce of his willpower to force himself to look away. After all, Delaney was breastfeeding a baby who might theoretically be his son.

Ryan listened, hearing the soft, gentle sounds of the baby nursing. Delaney's equally soft, gentle murmurings blended in to form a chorus he simply couldn't ignore.

"If I agree to the DNA test," she said, then paused a long time. "I'll have it done myself. I'd want the results to come to me."

Ryan waited for her to add more. But that was apparently it. No actual promise to do the test or even to share the information with him.

Not exactly the compromise he'd been hoping for.

Nor was it an acceptable one.

He glanced in the nursery again, to try to make eye contact with her so she'd know that he wasn't pleased. Delaney had a small blanket discreetly covering her breasts and most of Patrick's head. Ryan could see the child grabbing his toes.

There was only the possibility that this child was a product of a cloned embryo. A *small* possibility. Besides, he couldn't even consider it until he'd gotten past the first step. And the first step was to convince Delaney to do the DNA test.

"You might as well come in," she offered. "Seems a little late for modesty, doesn't it?"

It was a little late for a lot of things.

The doors of his heart seemed to be opening, and Ryan had no idea why they were doing that.

Or if he could even close them again.

He took a few steps closer, but he didn't actually enter the room. He stayed in the doorway. It was best to keep some physical distance between them, since he wasn't doing well in the emotional-distance department.

"You look shell-shocked. Did you get bad news with that phone call?" she asked.

"Not really." And since that was a lie, Ryan regrouped. "I did get *some* news. The New Hope clinic was located in the hospital where my son died." Thankfully, he'd managed to lay that out there without too much emotion in his voice.

Delaney made a sound of contemplation. Paused. And made another sound. A decidedly uneasy one. "It doesn't prove anything."

However, Ryan barely heard the words he'd already anticipated, because, at that exact moment, the baby shoved the blanket from his face. Delaney quickly covered her breast, sliding her stretchy top back in place.

Patrick turned his head in Ryan's direction, and just like that, their eyes connected.

His hair was blond. Light-colored wavy hair that haloed around his head. There was a tiny creamy white milk bubble at the corner of his mouth. He kicked his chubby legs and grinned. Just grinned. Showing his dimples. That grin made it all the way to his blue eyes.

Ryan's breath froze in his lungs.

Everything froze.

He couldn't move, couldn't speak. But he could feel. God, he could feel. The flood of emotion nearly brought him to his knees.

Because he knew.
Ryan just knew.
That this child was his son.

Chapter Seven

Delaney made sure her top and nursing bra were fixed so she wasn't flashing Ryan. Of course, Patrick didn't cooperate. He continued to bat at the blanket and her clothes, probably giving their visitor a peep show in the process.

She glanced at Ryan to see if he'd been embarrassed by the exposure, but her glance turned into a stare. That wasn't an embarrassed look on his face. He was stunned, truly stunned. So much so that he grabbed each side of the door frame and held on.

"What—" But that was all Delaney managed to say. She followed Ryan's wide-eyed gaze and saw what had captured his attention.

Patrick.

Delaney's eyes widened, as well.

And she didn't have to ask what was going on in Ryan's head. She knew. It was no doubt the same reaction she'd had the night she'd seen his son's photo.

"There's a resemblance," she said.

That was all she could manage. And it was a weak attempt to defuse what was happening. It was like an avalanche, coming right down on top at her.

Ryan wasn't faring much better. He stood there, holding on to the door until his knuckles turned white, while he blew out quick, frantic breaths.

Since Patrick no longer seemed interested in nursing, Delaney got up and eased him back into his crib. When he made a few sounds of protest, she turned on his overhead mobile. He immediately settled once the music started to play and the cartoon figures began to circle around.

"A thousand things are going through my head right now," she confessed. "And very few of those things are good."

Ryan just nodded. That didn't do much to steady her suddenly raw nerves. The tears were threatening, too, but Delaney choked them back.

"I can't lose my baby." Her whispered

admission cut through Patrick's cooing and the cheerful music coming from the mobile.

But she immediately regretted her fear-induced confession, because it was a stark reminder that Ryan had already lost his son.

Or had he?

Judging from his reaction, he no doubt believed his child was in the crib.

Unfortunately, she couldn't challenge that. Dr. Keyes had claimed that the cloning was only a possibility, but it wasn't a mere *possibility* that was causing Ryan to experience this turmoil. Patrick was the cause of it. His blond hair. His blue eyes. And his uncanny resemblance to the man standing in the doorway of the nursery.

Why hadn't she realized that there was some resemblance before now?

Why?

Probably because she hadn't wanted to see it.

As long as the experimentally cloned embryo was just a rumor and without a shred of proof to back it up, she was safe. Her son was safe.

However, nothing was safe any longer.

The perfect life she'd so carefully planned was coming apart at the seams, and she couldn't even blame Ryan for that. He'd had no part in making this happen. But then, neither had she. They weren't at fault, but both of them—and Patrick—would no doubt have to deal with the consequences.

"I need to know what you're thinking," she said when she could no longer stand his silence. She edged closer. Small steps. Afraid to get too near.

Ryan groaned softly, readjusted his position so that he was leaning against the nursery wall, probably for support. He definitely didn't look steady yet. "I'm thinking we need to do that DNA test."

That was it. No veiled threats about challenging her for custody of Patrick. No shouts or accusations that she should have told him that he and Patrick looked so much alike. Just those calmly spoken words that hit her as hard as a heavyweight's fist.

"And then what?" Delaney continued before he could answer. She *had* to make him understand. "My parents got married because my mom was pregnant with me.

They divorced just a year later. It probably won't come as a surprise to hear that we were dysfunctional. Lots of custody squabbles. Plenty of arguments. Both of them used me, always pulling, always manipulating until I swore that wouldn't happen to my child." Delaney paused. "Do you understand what I'm saying?"

Ryan's eyes darkened, and he seemed on the verge of shouting out the accusations she'd anticipated. But then something happened. Something changed. He stared at her, his eyes softening.

And then he reached out to her.

Delaney almost retreated, but Ryan hadn't reached out to her in anger. He skimmed his index finger down her right cheek, collecting the tear she didn't even know was there.

"Do you understand that I can't lose my son again?" he asked.

Definitely not a thunderous accusation. No anger whatsoever. But there was pain. Delaney could feel it. In him. In her. It was thick and real, unreachable, and yet it was there. Right there. And she had a sickening fear that it would get a lot worse before this was over.

There was also an equally sickening feeling that this would *never* be over.

"I nearly died when I lost them," he said, the grief all through his voice. "I *did* die."

With a sound of pure agony, Ryan stepped toward her. He slid his arm around her waist and pulled her to him. At first, Delaney couldn't figure out why he'd done that. Like the tear on her cheek, she hadn't been aware that she was actually wobbling. Probably on the verge of falling flat on her face. His grip prevented that from happening.

"I can't walk away from this," he whispered. "I can't pretend he isn't here."

"I know."

And she did know. Still, that didn't stop her heart from breaking. God, she could lose Patrick.

She could lose him.

Her breath shattered, a hoarse sob she couldn't stop. It came with the flood of fear and emotion.

"Shh," she heard Ryan say. He repeated it, his warm breath brushing over her hair and cheek.

He was actually comforting her. Or rather trying to. Although there wasn't much chance of his succeeding, she welcomed anything that wasn't this awful agony she was feeling.

Surprised by his tender gesture, she looked up at him.

And Delaney immediately realized that was a huge mistake.

Ryan looked down at the same time, and their gazes connected, met and held. Truly held. As they were staring at each other, at least a dozen things passed between them. Unsaid. But understood. There it was. All their uncertainties. Their concerns.

Shared emotions.

That created a camaraderie between them that Delaney was sure neither of them welcomed. But it was undeniably present.

"You should have never told me about the pocket watch," she whispered, figuring it wouldn't make any sense to him. But it made sense to her. She could totally understand his need to purchase something to recreate a past, a life that he'd never had.

The need to make things right.

She had that same need, and that was part of the reason she'd so desperately wanted a child.

"You shouldn't have told me about the butterfly." His voice barely had any sound, but she heard every word.

She shook her head, trying to clear it. It didn't help. It seemed as if the world turned on its axis. Everything moved a little off-kilter.

And so did Ryan.

So did she, for that matter.

His head dipped down, moving closer toward her. Stunned, unable to prevent what was happening, Delaney just stood there as his mouth came to hers.

Barely a touch.

And yet, it was much more than that.

So much more.

A rough sound rumbled in his throat. A protest, and one she definitely understood, because there was no logical reason for this to be happening.

But it *was* happening.

Their lips met. Warmth against warmth. Again, not a real kiss, but it suddenly seemed as if it were the most real kiss she'd ever experienced. Not born of passion. Well, not entirely anyway. But it was there.

Passion that she shouldn't be feeling.

That was a much-needed jolt that brought her back from this kiss-induced fantasy to the real world. She and Ryan had huge problems to work out, and those problems shouldn't involve kissing.

Ryan must have realized what she had at the same moment. He let go of her and stepped away.

Delaney did some retreating of her own. "I can't," she managed to say.

"I know. I can't, either."

Okay. So they were in agreement.

Good.

It was the only logical decision they could make. Yes, there was a weird attraction between them. Something sexual. But it was only a by-product of the intense emotion created by all the other issues they were dealing with. Nothing more. Just a normal response to the stress.

And Delaney was *almost* certain she believed that.

"We'll do the DNA test," she said, to end the silence between them and also prevent a discussion of the kiss.

He nodded, and he looked past her to the crib.

She knew he wanted to go closer for a

better look at Patrick. But despite the strange intimacy that had just occurred between them, she couldn't make the offer of allowing him to see her son.

Of course, she wouldn't stop him, either.

And Ryan took that noninvitation. He did venture closer. But he only made it a few steps before the loud pounding at the front door.

"Open up, Delaney!" someone called out.

But not just someone.

Her father.

Ryan's shoulders stiffened. "Is that who I think it is?"

She hated to confirm it, but she knew Ryan had probably recognized the voice. After all, they'd had their share of encounters. "Yes."

Ryan mumbled something and immediately stepped around her, obviously headed for the door.

Definitely not a good idea.

She caught his arm. "If we don't answer it, he might go away. I don't know about you, but I'm not ready for another emotional upheaval right now."

Ryan stopped, obviously debating what to do. But his thoughts were interrupted and overshadowed by the shouts, profanity and constant pounding.

"I know he's in there," her father yelled.

That comment did a thorough job of robbing Delaney of what little composure she'd managed to regain.

"McCall?" Richard Nash challenged. "Get out here now, or I'll break down the damn door."

Her grip on Ryan's arm wasn't enough to hold him back. He broke free and headed straight toward what would almost certainly be an ugly, and possibly violent, confrontation with her father.

Chapter Eight

Ryan hadn't thought that this particular visit could get any more difficult, but he'd obviously been wrong. The man at Delaney's door would definitely complicate things at a time when they needed no more complications.

What he should be doing was convincing Delaney to have the DNA test done right away, before she could change her mind. He should be trying to soothe the pain that was in her eyes. And finally—he should be introducing himself to the little boy cooing and babbling in the baby bed. Instead, he was apparently on a familiar collision course with a man who seemed determined to make his life a living hell.

Ryan stormed toward the front door, Delaney right behind him. She was pleading with him to go back into the nursery, a place he truly wanted to be. But there was no way he could let Delaney face her mentally unstable father alone. Especially since Richard Nash's latest threat didn't seem to be aimed only at Delaney but at him.

Get out here now, or I'll break down the damn door.

Ryan saved the man the trouble of doing that. While Nash was still making threats, Ryan yanked open the door and faced an obviously enraged man.

"McCall," her father said, barely sparing Delaney a glance. Everything about the man exuded anger. His narrow, light green eyes. The rigid muscles in his face. His soldier-stiff posture. He was obviously primed and ready for a fight.

Ryan positioned himself in front of Delaney in case there *was* a fight. It certainly wouldn't be the first time that he and Nash had come to blows. It'd happened the day after Ryan had gained control of Nash's company. Nash had confronted him in the parking lot and had even managed to connect his right fist with Ryan's jaw. Ryan had stopped the fight from escalating, restrained him so that security could haul the man away. And then hours later, Nash had attempted suicide.

Since he and Delaney had more important issues—Patrick—Ryan didn't intend for things to go in a violent direction today. He somehow needed to defuse the situation quickly so that they wouldn't waste precious time.

"You have no right," Nash snarled.

Ryan was about to ask for clarification on that all-encompassing accusation when Delaney stepped around him. "What are you doing here?" Not exactly a snarl like her father's. More like a plea that he leave immediately.

But Nash showed no signs of moving, or even responding to his daughter's question. He stayed firmly planted on the porch. Planted and imposing.

It didn't matter that the man was in his mid-fifties, Richard Nash was still a formidable foe. Other than threads of gray in his dark brown hair, there were few signs of age. He was well over six feet tall and at least two hundred and fifty pounds. His body hadn't gone to fat, either. Nash was in better shape than most men half his age.

And Ryan had no doubt that Nash would be willing to use all that physical strength against him.

Or even Delaney.

"Why am I here? I could ask your *guest* the same thing," Nash countered. "How could you have done this to me, Delaney? *How?* You know what he is. You know what he did to me. And yet he's here, in your house."

With each word, the veins in Nash's neck became more visible. Practically bulging. And that was Ryan's cue to get Delaney out of the line of fire. He stepped between them again. However, that didn't stop Delaney from asking her father another question.

"How did you know Ryan was here?"

It was a good question, too, one that Ryan wished he'd thought of. Unfortunately, he didn't like any of the answers that came to mind.

Nash's mouth tightened, and he volleyed acidic glances between the two of them. "Someone called me and said they saw McCall pull up in front of your house."

Delaney made a sound to indicate she didn't believe him. Ryan didn't, either.

Nash was apparently as inept at business as he was at telling a lie.

"You were watching Delaney," Ryan accused.

His accusation caused Nash a few moments of debate before he finally challenged Ryan's icy gaze with one of his own. "Maybe. Didn't you think I'd find out you were seeing her? That car accident was all over the newspapers."

"Seeing her?" Ryan repeated.

Okay. So that's what this little visit was about.

Or was it?

Was that particular assumption meant to distract them from the point that Nash had obviously been keeping tabs on his daughter? And if so, how long had Nash been doing that? Since the car incident that'd nearly killed them?

Or even before that?

If so, Richard Nash could have been the driver of the vehicle.

It was a reasonable concern, especially since Nash hadn't even bothered to ask Delaney if she'd been hurt. That was something most fathers would have wanted to know. Not Nash, though.

"There's nothing going on between Ryan and me," Delaney explained.

That shakily delivered denial obviously didn't please her father, probably because she'd used Ryan's given name. Or maybe Nash was simply riled because Delaney and he were side-by-side and facing down the man who had nothing but hatred in his eyes.

Hatred for both of them.

Delaney shook her head. "We're not involved. Not like you think."

"He's here, isn't he? Standing right next to you. God, you even smell like him." Nash cursed. It was raw and vicious. Then, with his teeth together, his focus still on his daughter, he said. "I'd rather see you dead and in hell than involved with the likes of Ryan McCall."

That did it. Ryan didn't intend to stand there any longer while the man threatened Delaney. "It's time for you to leave," Ryan warned. He'd back up the warning with force if necessary.

Nash turned in Ryan's direction. Nothing quick. But a slow, calculated turn. Like the reaiming of a lethal weapon. It didn't deter Ryan. He was the master at staring people down. And he'd do whatever was necessary to get Richard Nash out of there. The man obviously posed a threat to Delaney and therefore to Patrick.

That kind of threat wasn't unacceptable.

It fed the emotions and the rage that Ryan battled with daily. The rage over losing his wife and son. He wouldn't just stand by and let that happen again. Even if Delaney wasn't his wife, she was someone he felt compelled to protect.

Ryan walked closer to Nash and ignored Delaney when she clamped her fingers on his arm. *"You're leaving now,"* Ryan said to her father.

Despite his obvious size advantage, Nash actually dropped back a step. No surprise there. Ryan's threat wasn't a bluff. It was as real as the dangerous energy bubbling inside him. An energy that threatened to break free.

"This isn't over," Nash said.

But he took another step back.

"Yes. It is," Ryan countered.

Another step. And another. Until Nash nearly stumbled off the porch. He tossed out more profanity, most of it aimed at Delaney, and some of it just a generic blast of verbal anger directed at life in general. Finally he turned and hurried toward his car parked in front of Delaney's house.

Ryan never took his attention from the man. He stood in the doorway and watched until Nash drove away.

"That wasn't necessary," he heard Delaney say.

Because Ryan was still caught up in the adrenaline of the battle he'd just fought, it took him a few seconds to realize she wasn't pleased.

He shut the door, locked it and looked at her. "He threatened you."

"So?" She lifted her hands, palms up, in the air. "He threatens me a lot, about everything. And about nothing. Besides, it's better to have him direct his anger at me than you."

Ryan had to work hard to keep his mouth from dropping open. "And how do you figure that?"

"He's never acted on those threats."

"There's always a first time. And maybe that first time has already happened."

She blinked. "What do you mean?"

Ryan hadn't intended to bring this up now. But even though it wasn't an ideal time, Delaney had to know what he suspected. "Your father could have been responsible for the road incident. He could have seen us driving together, and he might have wanted to show his *disapproval* by putting us in that ditch."

She was shaking her head even before he finished. "He wouldn't hurt me."

"He already has, Delaney. You're a nervous wreck." To prove his point, he took her hand and showed her that her fingers were trembling.

"That reaction's not solely because of my father." She pulled her hand from his, turned and headed back toward the nursery.

Ryan filled in the blanks. He was partly responsible for what she was going through. In fact, perhaps more so than her father. Because if her father often threatened her, she might be immune to it.

Even though God knows how.

But she wouldn't be immune to the questions he'd raised about her son. Those questions no doubt threatened her in the worse way possible.

Feeling lower than dirt for adding to her misery, Ryan followed her to the nursery. She held on to the side of the crib, gripping it hard, and stared down at Patrick. When Ryan walked closer, he realized the baby had fallen back to sleep. With all the shouting, it was a surprise that Patrick hadn't started crying.

That riled him.

No child should have to go through something like that. The shouting. The fighting. The anger. And he should know. He'd endured years of it living in foster care and with distant relatives who didn't want him around.

"My father doesn't come here often," Delaney said. "In fact, his last visit was before Patrick was born."

It wasn't much of a consolation.

Besides, an infrequent upheaval was still an upheaval. Something neither she nor Patrick needed in their lives.

Ryan joined her, and he stared down into the crib. Despite the emotion and turmoil caused by Nash's visit, one look at that face, and Ryan lost his anger and fury.

Talk about a cure for all kinds of things.

Even though he had no proof that this little boy was his son, the bond was already there. Or maybe it was simply a matter of *wanting* to protect Patrick.

And Delaney.

His need to keep her safe was as strong as it was for the little boy who lay sleeping. Ryan wanted to blame it on the kiss that shouldn't have happened.

That shouldn't have felt the way it did.

And it sure as heck shouldn't have been that memorable.

Along with the pleasure from the kiss, he'd also gotten a hefty dose of guilt. Until today, about a half hour ago, he'd considered himself a married man. Ironic, since technically he hadn't been married since Sandra died. However, his heart and soul had never quite grasped that technicality.

Until that kiss.

It had changed everything.

"Should we do the DNA test while he's asleep?" Delaney whispered.

But she didn't wait for him to answer. A good thing, too. Because she'd managed to surprise him yet again.

She reached into his jacket pocket and extracted the kit. Ryan didn't trust his voice to say anything. Not that he would have known what to say anyway. *Thank you* didn't seem nearly adequate.

He watched as she took the swab, slipped

it into Patrick's mouth and rubbed it against the inside of his cheek. Patrick stirred a little, making sounds of protest, and his chubby fist swatted at the intrusion. However, the moment Delaney took it from his mouth, he settled back into a peaceful sleep.

She placed the swab back into the plastic bag, but instead of handing it to Ryan, she placed it on the changing table next to the crib. "I'll have the test done, and I'll let you know the results."

And she would.

Ryan didn't doubt that.

But by doing the test solo, it also meant Delaney had to deal with the outcome—alone. Not his first choice for the way things should happen, but he didn't think she would budge on this.

"The address of the lab is on the bag," he said. "If you want to use some other place, that's fine."

She nodded and looked away.

Oh, yeah. This was ripping her to pieces, and after that kiss, Ryan wasn't sure she'd appreciate any attempt by him to comfort her. Besides, he might have succeeded in getting her to do the DNA test, but there was another equally important matter to be dealt with.

"Do you believe what happened the other night was really an accident?" he asked. Hopefully, it was a start to what would be a persuasive argument.

Delaney stared at him. "I want to believe it, but I just don't know."

Good. She had doubts, and that was progress. Now, for step two. "Even if your father wasn't behind the wheel of that car, someone was. And you know what? It might not matter if the person was out to get you, me, or both of us."

She frowned. "Is there a point to all of this?"

"Absolutely. I don't think it's safe for you to stay here alone." Ryan watched his words register. By degrees. Degrees that clearly didn't please her.

"You said you had enemies. If the person is after you, then…" She stopped.

Ryan hoped they'd just made a huge leap of progress.

"That's a huge *if,* isn't it, Delaney?" he asked. "It's also an unnecessary chance to take. A chance I don't want you to take."

"Because of Patrick," she finished.

"And because of you."

Oh, yeah.

That registered all right.

Delaney sank down into the rocking chair. "This is about that kiss, isn't it? Well, it shouldn't be. That was an adrenaline reaction. Nothing more. You hear that? *Nothing. More.* I won't let it cloud my judgment or cause me to do something I shouldn't do."

Maybe if she repeated it enough, one of them would start to believe it.

Not him, of course.

But Delaney could perhaps convince herself.

"Adrenaline, huh?" Ryan repeated. That was as good a reason as any. "But a kiss doesn't change the issues of security, and you've got some huge issues."

She gave a crisp, all-right nod. "I'll call Sheriff Knight. Maybe he can provide police protection. If not, then maybe SAPD can."

"I have a better idea." Ryan hoped it sounded like a better idea to Delaney when she heard it. "Patrick and you could stay at my estate."

The room went totally silent.

He could see the argument, or rather *arguments,* already forming in her eyes, so Ryan did a preemptive strike. Because this was an argument she couldn't win. "Play worst-case scenario. Even if the accident was directed at me, your father could return. What if he barges in here? He's enraged, and you can't reason with an enraged man."

She opened her mouth, probably to challenge him, but Ryan just forged ahead. "And even if the police can provide you with protection, it'd be minimal. Probably a cruiser patrolling the area. Not exactly an ideal solution."

Delaney gave him an uh-huh look. "And what *you're* offering *is* ideal?"

"I have the best security system that money can buy. The entire perimeter of the estate is rigged with motion detectors and alarms. I can hire guards to man the gate. You'll be safe." He rested on the arms of her chair and leaned in. "Patrick will be safe. I promise you."

She shook her head.

"Don't think about how wrong that kiss was," Ryan continued. "Don't let that be the deciding factor in this. The estate is huge. Plenty of room for both Patrick and you. All you have to do is take what I'm offering."

Delaney moved his hand aside and got up. She didn't just get up—she sprang out of the chair. "I can't. Don't you understand? I can't."

Ryan was about to assure her that he wouldn't take no for an answer. But Delaney did a preemptive strike of her own.

"I'm not thinking about how *wrong* that kiss was, Ryan," she said, scooping Patrick into her arms. She headed for the door. "I'm thinking about how *right* it felt."

WELL, THAT WAS a real Pandora's-box kind of confession, and Delaney was already mentally kicking herself before she even made it out of the nursery.

Could she possibly have said anything more stupid?

But unfortunately, it was the truth. Her body was still humming from that kiss, and she wasn't the sort of person to hum.

Before Ryan McCall had appeared in her life, she hadn't missed being in a man's arms. She hadn't missed the intimacy of simply being held.

Well, she missed it now.

She could thank Ryan, her suddenly needy body and her ridiculous confession for that.

"Did you think I'd just let that pass?" she heard Ryan say.

Delaney sighed because he was right on her heels. Not that she'd expected him to stay put. She'd all but offered him carte blanche to strip off her clothes and have sex with her.

And why did that suddenly seem like an irresistible, tantalizing idea?

Because she was obviously losing it, that's why.

The stress had gotten to her, though it didn't seem like stress. It seemed more like a hungry need for a man she shouldn't be needing.

Ryan managed to step ahead of her before she could make it into the kitchen. The overtaking wouldn't have bothered Delaney so much if it hadn't put them face-to-face. After she'd humiliated herself, eye contact was the last thing she wanted.

"The kiss felt right to me, too," he admitted. "Which, of course, also means it was wrong."

"Oh, no. Not this." She slapped her hand on his chest to keep him from moving closer. "Look, we can't both be insane at the same time. We have to take turns or something. And right now, it's my turn, okay?"

Needing something between them, Delaney repositioned Patrick, who was still sleeping. It didn't help. The dangerous energy was there, zipping back and forth between Ryan and her.

"You think I wanted that kiss to feel the way it did?" Ryan continued. He shook his head. "Okay, bad question. I *did* want it to feel that way. I can't completely ignore the fact that I'm a man and you're a woman. Laws of attraction and—"

"We shouldn't be discussing this."

He ignored her. Another head shake. He mumbled something under his breath. "I think about you when I shouldn't be thinking about you, Delaney. And in my mind, I've already kissed you at least a dozen times."

That confession took her breath away. It simply vanished. Lack of breath definitely didn't help her battle the fantasies of him that she was trying to push aside. "You have?"

"I have." He stepped closer. Touched the back of her hand. Rubbed softly with his thumb. "I knew the feel of you. The taste of you. How you'd fit in my arms. How we'd fit together. I knew all of that before I ever touched you."

Good grief. Much more of this, and she'd have to start fanning herself. Or take him off to bed. Mercy. Her body was starting to soften and burn. Preparing itself for something it wouldn't get.

And her body wouldn't get Ryan.

"But the truth is, before today, I hadn't kissed a woman since my wife died," he continued. "I hadn't *wanted* to kiss a woman. And I'm having a lot of trouble dealing with that."

Because Delaney was trying to block all that heat and sizzle, she also attempted to block out what he was saying but couldn't. "You haven't been with anyone since then?"

"No."

She felt some of the frustration drain away. And worse, she felt another connection with him. First the pocket watch, then the butterfly search. Now, this.

"Some pair we are," she mumbled. "We're

not exactly poster material for active sex lives."

The corner of his mouth lifted. "It's been a long time for you?"

"Oh, yeah." And Delaney was sorry she'd admitted that so quickly. But what the heck. Part of her wanted to share the misery in his eyes. At least, she wanted to share something. Better misery than another kiss. "I broke up with my last boyfriend over two years ago. I wanted children. He didn't. He left."

"You were in love with him?"

She shrugged. "I think I was in love with the idea of having a family. It's what I've always wanted, and he didn't have any desire to be part of that."

And they were back to Patrick. It didn't dilute the effect of the sensations inside her body, but it got her mind back to where it belonged.

"Please understand that I can't go to your estate," she told him. "Especially after that kiss. My instincts tell me to distance myself from you."

"Which instincts are those?"

"Not the ones involving sexual fantasies, that's for sure."

She'd meant to say that as a saucy, sarcastic comeback, but it sort of backfired. Ryan's mouth quivered. The right corner lifted.

And he smiled.

Mercy. That was an unexpected weapon in his male arsenal. The man had dimples. Actual dimples. The kind that looked more at home on movie-star heartthrobs. Not good. He was already attractive enough without adding something wholesome like dimples to the mix.

Or honesty.

And the man was indeed honest. Many of things he'd just admitted to her were better left unsaid yet he'd said them. That dimple-enhanced candor was probably the greatest aphrodisiac of all.

Since she was quickly losing ground, and since her arms were starting to tire from holding Patrick, Delaney checked around for the infant seat that she normally kept on the floor next to the dining table.

It wasn't there.

Only then did she remember she'd left it in her car, which was parked in her garage. She'd taken both the seat and Patrick to the day-care center that morning and had used it for him while she went through some correspondence. Her options now were to get past Ryan and head for the nursery and the crib.

But stepping around him would almost certainly involve some body contact.

That meant going in the other direction, to the garage. With Patrick, because she wasn't about to hand him over to Ryan.

"I'll be right back," she said.

Of course, he followed her through the kitchen and into the laundry room.

"What will it take for me to convince you to stay at my home?" Ryan asked.

"A lot more than you've provided so far." Delaney balanced Patrick in her arms and threw open the door that led to the garage. Since it was as dark as a tomb, she flicked on the light switch.

Nothing.

She shook her head. This was just not her day.

However, the frustration and the remainder of her argument with Ryan died on her lips when she caught the scent of something that shouldn't have been in the garage.

Ryan obviously smelled it as well because he grabbed her shoulder and muscled his way in front of her.

It wasn't a second too soon.

There was a burst of orangy-red light. Flames, she quickly realized. They erupted without sound. Jolting over the back-end of her car and higher.

God, her garage was on fire.

Delaney tightened her grip on Patrick, sheltering his face against her chest so he wouldn't inhale the smoke and fumes. Ryan took her instinctive moves a step further and pushed her back into the laundry room.

He didn't waste any time. He snatched a towel from the laundry basket and went toward the flames. Delaney hurried back into the kitchen for the fire extinguisher that she kept beneath the sink. It was probably too small, but it'd be a better defense than the towel.

What she saw when she made it back to the garage sent her heart into her throat.

In those few short seconds that she'd been gone, the fire had tripled in size. Thick, choking coils of smoke scattered around them, fanning out everywhere. In every corner. The smoke, flames and the heat coming right at her.

"Ryan!" she called out. The sound of her voice startled Patrick, and he awoke with a jolt and started to cry.

When Ryan looked back at her, she tossed him the extinguisher and reached for the phone mounted on the wall to call 911. While she provided the info to the emergency operator, she heard Ryan spray the foam onto the flames.

Delaney prayed it would put out the fire. If not, it could spread, and she could lose her home.

And worse.

Much worse.

She peered back around the door frame to check on Ryan. The extinguisher had obviously done its job. And so had he. He was spraying with one hand and using the towel to bash out the rest. His efforts didn't stop the smoke and the ash, however. It was still there in abundance, and Ryan wasn't immune to it, either. He started to cough.

"Get Patrick outside," he yelled. "Into the backyard."

Because she couldn't risk her son's life, Delaney did as Ryan said. Cradling Patrick against her, she hurried back through the kitchen and onto her back porch.

She came to a dead stop when it suddenly occurred to her why Ryan had said the backyard and not the *front*. Maybe there was someone out there. Near the front door of her garage. Someone responsible for the fire that Ryan was fighting.

Oh, God.

Patrick must have sensed the danger and her reaction to it because his sobs increased in both volume and intensity. Delaney put her mouth against his tearsoaked cheek and kissed him. She murmured soft, hopefully soothing things to help him calm down. It worked on her son, but not on her.

Her heart was pounding, and the thoughts going through her head were not good. This was the stuff of nightmares.

She heard footsteps behind her and whirled around. Trying to brace herself for whatever she might face. Preparing herself for a possible fight.

But it was Ryan.

He was all right.

Well, for the most part.

Soot covered, his clothes singed and looking battle worn, he hurried onto the porch with her. "I managed to put out the fire," he said in between taking huge gulps of air. "But we should have the fire department check it just in case."

"Thank you." Though from the heart, Delaney knew those words weren't nearly enough. "If we hadn't seen the flames when we did, the fire would have made it into the house."

Ryan didn't confirm that, but Delaney knew it was true. The flames would have spread, destroying whatever, or whomever, was in their path. If she'd been in the nursery with Ryan, it might have been too late to save anything.

Including themselves.

Making a vigilant sweeping survey of the redwood-fenced yard, he took her arm and moved her off the porch. Not far. He positioned Patrick and her between a sprawling oak and her rose garden. Not too far from the house, but not too close either in case the fire re-erupted. He didn't stop there. As he'd done with her father, and in the garage, Ryan placed himself between them and the gate—the only exterior entrance to the yard.

"You've made a habit of coming to the rescue," she whispered.

He swiped his forehead with the back of his hand. "Lucky timing."

But was it?

She was twenty-nine years old, and before the meeting with Ryan at his estate, she'd never been in a car accident and never experienced a fire in her home. Now, both had happened within the past two days. Even if she wanted to believe in coincidence, and she *did*, it simply didn't feel like one.

"He's okay, right?" Ryan asked, tipping his head toward Patrick.

"He's fine."

Ryan reached out. To touch Patrick, she realized when she saw the direction his hand was moving. But he stopped and glanced down at the soot and grime on his fingers. Patrick watched the entire encounter with his complete attention centered on Ryan.

And then something happened.

Amid all the surging adrenaline and the rushed breaths, amid all the fear, Patrick's teary eyes went to Ryan's. A long, lingering, inquisitive look. Then, Patrick smiled as if he knew this man had just saved the day.

"Magic, huh?" Delaney managed to say,

though she did have to speak around the sudden lump in her throat.

"Hmm." And that was all Ryan said for several moments. In the distance, Delaney could hear the sirens from the fire truck. It wouldn't be long now before she could be reassured that the flames were completely out.

"Please tell me you don't intend to stay here after this," Ryan said, his voice raspy from the smoke and the coughing. He stared at her.

No. *Glared* at her.

He was daring her to defy him now.

"Let me rephrase that. You *can't* stay here, Delaney. It wouldn't just be stupid. It'd be dangerous."

She wanted to argue. Or better yet, she wanted to come up with some other solution. But until the police investigated this latest incident, they probably wouldn't be able to provide her with protection. And even then, she was willing to bet that the protection would be paltry compared to what Ryan could offer her.

And Patrick.

Ryan would definitely keep him safe.

Her son was her number-one priority.

Her *only* priority. To protect him, she had to swallow her pride. Her fears. And her concerns about Ryan.

Even if that would put them literally under his roof.

Where she couldn't possibly distance herself from him.

But Delaney had to wonder—how soon would it be before she seriously regretted her decision to accept Ryan's help?

Chapter Nine

Ryan had been right when he'd told her that his estate was massive, and even *massive* was an understatement.

Delaney hadn't noticed much about the place during her other visit, but she noticed now. The main house was three floors, and it was sprawling. Twenty-two rooms, Ryan had told her, surrounded by six hundred acres.

And it all belonged to him.

"This is a working ranch," Ryan said as he escorted Patrick and her inside the house. "If you're interested in riding, that can be arranged. There's also a pool and a gym."

Delaney mumbled thanks, something she'd been doing a lot during the drive to the estate and their walk inside.

Patrick seemed as awestruck with the

place as Delaney did. Her son's curious gaze slid from one part of the house to the other.

"Come this way," Ryan instructed, leading them up the stairs. "While we were at the police station giving our statements about the fire, I called Lena Sanchez, my household manager. I asked her to set up a nursery."

They went past the door to his office, a room Delaney definitely remembered. It was where all of this had started. If she'd never come that night, Ryan probably wouldn't have heard about the cloning rumors, and she wouldn't be here now.

They went down a hall, the walls lined with expensive-looking Native American rugs and artwork. Delaney tried not to gawk and finally just gave up and stared anyway.

"I know what you're thinking," Ryan commented, glancing back at her.

Delaney nodded. "Yes. This place is incredible."

Judging from Ryan's suddenly furrowed brow, her response was a surprise. "I figured you were thinking about how many businesses I'd taken over to be able to afford all of this."

No. That hadn't crossed her mind.

But it should have.

After all, Ryan had been her father's enemy for years, and yet here she'd walked into his lavish home and hadn't given the old issues even a passing thought.

Progress, maybe.

Or maybe his recent knightly deeds had blinded her to a lot of things.

"I inherited the place from my great-uncle about five years ago," Ryan explained. He pointed to a portrait on the wall, and judging from the resemblance, it was the relative they were discussing.

"But I thought you didn't know your family."

"Oh, I knew a few of them, Uncle Jess included. I even lived here for two weeks when I was ten. I was in between court hearings to determine placement, and the social worker goaded Uncle Jess into taking me." He paused, and a muscle jumped in his jaw. "It didn't work out."

"Still, he left you this place," Delaney said softly.

Ryan shrugged. "Only because he left no will and by then no other living relatives. I got the estate by default."

Yet Ryan had accepted the inheritance anyway. Not because he needed the money. Delaney did the math; and Ryan would have been twenty-seven then. Married to a wealthy heiress, and thanks to some highly lucrative and risky investments in real estate, he was already wealthy in his own right.

"Accepting this place was like trying to recreate your family history?" she asked, repeating what he'd told her earlier about the pocket watch.

The corner of his mouth lifted. "Something like that."

Ryan stopped and opened one of the doors. He stepped aside so that Delaney could enter first, and it didn't take her long to realize this was the nursery. Like Patrick's room at her house, it had a crib, a rocking chair and a changing table.

But that's where the similarities ended.

Size aside—and it was huge—there were stuffed animals—dozens of them—arranged neatly throughout the room. And toys. Trains, basketballs and other assorted playthings that weren't age appropriate for Patrick, but since her son's eyes widened even more, they obviously captured his attention.

Patrick reached for a bright blue bunny-shaped rattle on the changing tray, and he practically wiggled out of her arms to get it.

"For the record, none of this belonged to Adam," Ryan explained. He picked up the rattle and handed it to Patrick. Her son thanked him with a squeaky giggle and promptly began to bop Ryan and himself with the toy. Finally, Patrick managed to stuff half of a bunny ear into his mouth.

"And this wasn't Adam's room," Ryan continued. "Lena made calls to a few department stores and arranged for immediate delivery of some things." He surveyed the room. "She obviously got a little carried away."

"Obviously." And while Delaney appreciated the household manager's effort to make her son feel at home, it didn't exactly put her at ease.

"This is a temporary arrangement," Delaney reminded him.

Ryan's gaze slashed to hers. "My motives aren't sinister. All I want is to make sure Patrick and you are comfortable and *safe.*"

And with that, Ryan walked across the

nursery and threw open a door. "Your room's in here. I thought you'd like to stay close to Patrick. There's a monitor on your nightstand so you can hear and watch him at all times. If you need a break, Lena has volunteered to step in as nanny. *Temporary* nanny," he amended.

Ryan proceeded to point out the bathroom and the closet of her suite in a tone that had definitely cooled.

Delaney touched Ryan's arm when he started toward the door on the opposite side of the room. "I really do appreciate all of this."

He nodded, paused and nodded again. "You have every reason in the world to distrust me. The truth is—I did a hostile takeover of your father's manufacturing company. And not because I especially wanted or needed it. It was just another conquest. What I did wasn't illegal, but that didn't make it right, either. I'm sorry for that."

The admission should have made Delaney feel a lot better. An apology, something she'd thought she'd never hear from Ryan. However, like the well-stocked nursery, it sent an uneasy feeling through her.

It took a moment for her to realize why.

The bitterness in their past was a fierce barrier between them. A barrier she needed, after the way she'd responded to the brief encounter in his arms. With that particular obstruction gone, Delaney had to wonder what would stop her now from falling hard for this man who could ultimately take everything from her?

And the answer was—*nothing* would stop her.

Whether she wanted it to happen or not, she was already falling hard for Ryan McCall.

"SO THE FIRE WAS ARSON," Ryan concluded after listening to his security manager's report.

"The police are still investigating," Quentin explained, "but all signs point to it being purposely set. Obvious signs, too. It appears the perpetrator soaked some rags with paint thinner and then ran about thirty yards of twine outside the garage. A makeshift fuse. Amateurish but effective."

Definitely. And potentially lethal. "What about witnesses? Did any of Delaney's neighbors see anything?"

"No. The cops are still checking on Richard Nash though, and they gave me the standard line—they're looking for evidence, suspects, etc. etc."

It wasn't nearly enough. The fire had been a real wake-up call. He needed to get to the bottom of what was happening before things escalated. And, unfortunately, Ryan was afraid things would escalate soon.

"You want me to pay a visit to Richard Nash, have a chat with him?" Quentin asked.

"No." Ryan didn't even have to think about that. He'd leave Delaney's father to the cops for now. Their history could have Nash claiming foul play. Maybe the police could find some kind of physical evidence to link the man to the fire. That would tie everything up in a neat little package.

But Ryan couldn't count on that happening.

Something in his gut told him there'd be no neat packages for this one.

"Tomorrow afternoon I have an appointment with the director of the New Hope clinic, Dr. Emmett Montgomery," Ryan told Quentin. "He might have answers that'll help with all of this."

Questioning Dr. Montgomery was a long shot, but it was a possibility that Ryan couldn't overlook. Richard Nash was the obvious culprit, but he wasn't the only one. Ryan didn't intend to ignore the theory that the fire and the car accident might have been warnings to send Delaney running. A woman on the run wouldn't be able to answer questions about the New Hope clinic's wrongdoings.

Wrongdoings.

Not really an appropriate word, considering that it might have brought back his son.

Ryan had resisted it for hours, but no longer. Trying to suppress his guilt, he turned on the monitor next to his bed, and the video feed of the nursery popped onto the screen. Just like that, with the flick of a button, he had a perfect view of Patrick asleep in the crib. The little boy was tucked in for the night.

As he'd done at Delaney's house, Ryan studied the precious little face. A bizarre kind of torment. While the face was so genetically similar to his own, this was not a child he could claim totally as his own.

Yet, he couldn't let Patrick go, either.

Ryan adjusted the angle of the video feed and waited. He listened carefully and thought he might have heard Delaney's shower running, which meant it wouldn't be long before she came back into the nursery to check on him.

Ryan didn't even try to stop himself. Like watching the monitor, it was a battle he'd lose. Instead, he used the adjoining door of his suite. A door that led directly into the nursery. It was a security precaution.

Among other things.

Security, because he hadn't wanted Patrick or Delaney to be too far away from him. However, his concerns weren't all security related. One look at the child in the crib, and Ryan knew that was true.

And that his feelings didn't just apply to Patrick, either.

No.

They applied to Delaney, as well.

And that didn't please him.

Delaney and Patrick weren't his for the taking. Besides, even if Delaney wanted him in her life, and that, too, was unlikely, Ryan couldn't take that risk again. She might have awakened something inside him, but he was certain other parts of him, including his heart, had been buried right along with Sandra and Adam.

For everyone's sake, he needed to maintain a status quo. He couldn't go through that pain again.

Ryan reached down and lightly brushed his fingers over Patrick's hair. It felt like tiny threads of gold silk. Definitely not a status quo kind of feeling.

"Is he still asleep?"

The voice startled him, and Ryan jerked back his hand as if he'd been caught raiding the cookie jar. He reeled around and saw Delaney in the doorway of her bedroom.

She'd obviously just finished her shower. Her hair was still damp, lying against the tops of her shoulders. Even in the dimly lit room, Ryan could see that her face was flushed, probably from the heat of the hot water.

He felt himself flush, too. Definitely not from a shower, but from the immediate effect she had on him. His reaction to Delaney was quickly becoming a conditioned response. All he had to do was look at her, think of her, and all sorts of bad thoughts popped into his head.

Like now, for instance.

Even though he'd only kissed her once, he was having no trouble filling in the blanks of how it would feel to take that kiss one step farther. Okay, a lot of steps farther. So far that they wouldn't be able to stop with just a kiss.

How would she respond to his kiss? To his touch? And how would it feel to make love to her? No. Not *make love*. That implied something gentle and controlled. A leisurely pace. His desire for her wasn't of the controlled, leisurely variety. It was more in the take-her-now category. An urgency. A need so overwhelming that Ryan caught on to the crib to stop himself from moving toward her.

Oh, man. He wanted her.

Judging from the smile she offered him, she had no idea of the lecherous thoughts on his mind. If she did, she'd have turned and run in the other direction.

But she didn't run. Cinching her silky emerald-green bathrobe around her, she walked closer, bringing the scent of the soap, shampoo and *her.* It was a combination that went straight through him. Like a double shot of expensive whiskey.

Ryan gripped the crib railing even harder. He was *so* in trouble here.

"He's still asleep?" she repeated.

Ryan nodded and forced himself to breathe so he could talk. "The question is—for how long?"

"Probably through the night. A recent occurrence. Lately, he's been skipping his two a.m. feeding." She looked around. "Your room must be nearby. I checked the monitor before I got in the shower. You weren't here then, and I only stayed in the shower a minute or two."

Feeling even more like a cookie thief, Ryan hitched his thumb to the other adjoining door. "I have a monitor, as well."

She nodded and took a deep breath. "You're concerned about something going wrong."

"Yes. But you'll be all right here at the estate. I just didn't want to be too far out of earshot in case…well, just in case."

Delaney joined him at the crib. But she didn't just join him. She stood right next to him. Her arm brushed against his. "Part of me greatly appreciates that."

"And the other part?" he asked, not easily. His body seemed to be revving itself up for a long, satisfying bout of sex. Maybe they would be against the wall. On the floor. Hell, the location was optional. Except it wasn't. Because sex between them couldn't happen. And his brain knew that, so he pushed that revving aside.

"The other part of me wants to deny that there's any reason whatsoever for us to be paranoid."

Ryan tipped his head to Patrick. "There's our reason."

"All sixteen-and-a-half pounds of him," she whispered, smiling. She gave Patrick's blanket an adjustment that it didn't need and kissed his cheek. "He's growing so fast. Practically right before my eyes. And he seems to babble some new sound every day. When he strings all of those sounds and syllables together, it makes me wonder if we have a future rock star on our hands."

Her smile vanished. "On *my* hands," she corrected. Delaney adjusted the blanket again. "You think my father started the fire."

No more baby talk. Obviously, she wanted a change of subject because that *our* had spooked her. It'd actually unnerved him a little, too. Because it'd sounded a lot better than Ryan had ever imagined it would. He hadn't considered himself part of an *our* situation in a long, long time.

"Don't you think your father's responsible?" Ryan countered, forcing himself to take whatever turn Delaney wanted with this conversation.

"Maybe. But subterfuge isn't his strong suit. He's more of the in-your-face type. Besides, I'm not totally convinced he wants to kill me."

Ryan agreed. However, if Richard Nash wanted to hurt her, to punish her, he might end up accidentally killing her in the process.

"I plan to speak with Dr. Montgomery tomorrow afternoon," Ryan said. "If I get lucky, maybe Keyes will be there, too."

"If Lena can stay with Patrick, I'd like to go with you."

He angled his body so he could stare at her. "Lena could. If *I* wanted you to go with me. But I don't. If Keyes or Montgomery is behind these scare tactics, then it won't be safe for you to be around them."

Delaney huffed. "The doctors might not

talk to you. In fact, it's my guess that they'll claim patient confidentiality since they want to avoid discussing anything about the cloning. But if I'm there, they'll at least have to answer questions about my medical files."

She was right. Damn it. Still—

"If we go together," Delaney added, "it'll be safer. For both of us."

Ryan had already opened his mouth to object. Until she added that last part.

"What?" she challenged. "You think you're impervious to danger?"

He shook his head.

But he didn't think Delaney cared about his safety.

Oh, no.

No, no, no.

This couldn't be happening. He already had enough to deal with, with his revving body and its stupid demands. He didn't need Delaney to be concerned for him. Concern equaled feelings, and that would only add another layer to the already too-powerful sexual energy between them.

A bad layer.

One that could change erotic fantasies to making-love fantasies. Maybe he could handle the first, but the second was off-limits. He didn't have a choice about that.

She mumbled something under her breath and scooped her hand through her hair, pushing it away from her face. "Believe me, I don't like this any better than you do."

Ryan was almost afraid to ask, but he did anyway. "Are we talking about the visit to the clinic, or have we moved on to other things?"

She moistened her lips, mumbled something. "Other things."

"Oh."

Hell. Another of those proverbial layers. She was now pouring her heart out to him. Great. Just great. He should say goodnight, take a cold shower and go to bed. *Alone.* Because he was quickly losing ground here.

Delaney met his gaze and studied him a long time. "You look…"

"Uncomfortable?" he provided.

She considered that a moment and frowned. "No. You look interested."

Well, so much for hiding his feelings. And it was worse than that. She moistened her lips again, and Ryan felt his body clench and beg.

"I've really debated bringing this up," Delaney continued. "Let sleeping dogs lie and all of that. But the sleeping-dog approach isn't working. Well, not for me anyway." Judging from her frown, she wasn't pleased about it.

Neither was Ryan.

Really.

"Neither of us is the casual-affair type," she went on. "And an affair would be a truly stupid idea anyway. We have more important things to do than act on our libidos."

It was the most logical argument she could have made. There was just one problem with it. Logic didn't apply here, and it wasn't nearly enough to override the effects of the hormonal circus going on inside both of them.

He was sunk.

And heaven help him, he intended to keep on sinking.

Right now, he only wanted one thing, and she was standing right in from of him.

Ryan turned, facing her. "I am interested," he said. "And that sleeping-dog approach isn't working for me, either."

He quit thinking.

Quit analyzing.

He quit resisting.

And he acted. Fast. Because he didn't want anything to change his mind.

Ryan hooked his arm around her waist and pulled her to him. Against him. Not a gentle move. Mainly because she caught him, and her need seemed as urgent and burning as his own. The full body contact sent a jolt of fire through him. His heartbeat raced. His pulse was quick. His breath thin. And every part of him wanted her.

His mouth went to hers. As if he'd kissed her a thousand times. And it certainly felt that way, maybe because of those relentless fantasies he'd had about her. But for whatever reason, she tasted familiar. Like something he'd always desperately wanted. Like something forbidden. And of course, that only made it so much better.

He deepened the kiss. Deepened everything. Until he was beyond a place where reason and stopping made sense. Instead, he took. Claimed. Ravaged.

In the back of his mind, he realized this kiss, her taste, would stay with him forever.

If he ever kissed another woman, he would always and forever compare her to Delaney.

A staggering thought.

And still, it didn't stop him.

She lifted her arms, first one and then the other, and slid them around his neck. The adjustment in positions brought her right against him. Her breasts brushed against his chest. No bra. He knew that because he could feel her nipples on the other side of that silky fabric.

Ryan heard a primitive sound rumble in his chest, and he pulled her closer, tighter, against him. Her body, against his, until all he could feel was Delaney.

"This is wrong," she mumbled when they remembered they needed air to live. They broke the kiss, momentarily, and gulped in several huge breaths.

Stating the obvious, however, didn't stop them. Ryan immediately went back for more. Taking from her. Savoring all the sensations of her touch, her taste. Letting the kiss carry him to the only place he wanted to go.

And he wanted Delaney to go there with him.

"You're so good at this," she whispered against his mouth.

"That's not the best thing you can say to a man who's battling his willpower."

She pulled back slightly. The moonlight danced over his face. Over his body. "Are you still battling it?"

"No. I lost when you stepped into the room."

Her breath shuddered—a sound both erotic and totally feminine. She seemed to take his surrender as something to be tested. While he deepened the kiss, Delaney slid her body against his. Well, it was a little more than just a slide. It was an intimate caress. Her breasts moving against him. Her stomach. And especially her lower body.

He reacted.

Man, did he.

In the most human way that a man could react to a woman. He'd been battling his need since she walked into the room, but with that slide, that deep caress of their bodies, he lost the battle.

Delaney moaned. Shifted. She brushed against him and didn't back away. Just the opposite. She moved, into him, against him. Until Ryan dragged her even closer. Until they were plastered against each other.

Her hand moved to his chest. Stirring the muscles there. Not a gentle touch. Her fingers were seeking, exploring. But she didn't stop with his chest. She continued to touch. Continued to arouse. Sliding her fingers over to his side. A gliding caress that stirred him. Not that he needed anything else to stir him.

Delaney was enough.

Then, she stopped cold.

The muscles in her body tensed. Ryan realized she had her hand over his shoulder holster and his gun. A weapon he'd put on after the latest incident.

"It's just a safety measure," he said. Not easily. He was battling with both his breath and his composure.

She pulled open his jacket and looked inside. "That looks like a little more than a safety measure."

He braced himself for an admonishment, perhaps some kind of accusation that he'd sugarcoated the danger so it wouldn't worry her.

Which was exactly what he'd done.

But there was no accusation. Instead, her focus left the gun and went to the side pocket inside his jacket. Looking down, Ryan saw what had garnered her attention. The edge of the plastic bag was sticking up.

"The DNA test kit," Ryan explained. Not an explanation Delaney needed though since she obviously knew what it was. "I took it from the changing table at your house."

"Of course." She dropped back a step and wiped her mouth with her fingers. "You didn't have someone else take it to the lab?"

"No. Because you said you wanted to do that yourself."

"Yes." Another step back, and she nodded. "Go ahead. Send in the swab to be tested. I can't put this off any longer. It's not fair to either of us."

"Delaney—" Ryan reached for her, but she ducked around him.

"How soon will we know the results?"

This wasn't a conversation he wanted to have, but it obviously wasn't one he could avoid. "Maybe as early as tomorrow, if I have the lab expedite the test."

"Which you will," she said.

Delaney turned, ready to leave, but this time Ryan didn't let her go. He caught on to her, tried to comfort her and failed. Because unfortunately, he couldn't tell her that they'd skip the test. They needed to know the results, if for no other reason than to start dealing with the consequences. Still, that didn't make it easy.

She emitted a sound of frustration. "I'm scared you'll use the DNA results to try to take Patrick."

One sentence. That's all it took for her to nail what had been troubling both of them.

Ryan cupped her chin and ran his thumb over her bottom lip. It was damp and slightly swollen from the kissing war they'd just waged against each other. "That won't happen. I know what it's like to lose a child."

She studied his eyes, as if searching for the truth. Moments passed before she nodded, apparently satisfied that she'd just received the truth. Delaney brushed a kiss on his cheek.

Ryan couldn't have been more stunned if she'd slapped him.

That kiss wasn't the highly charged erotic exchange they'd had just minutes earlier. It was gentle. Soft. And intimate. In fact, it was as intimate as a kiss could be.

"Thank you for calming my fears about Patrick," she whispered, then turned and walked to her bedroom.

Ryan stood there, his body still burning, still wanting her. He waited for a thunderbolt from heaven to strike him for the probable lie he'd just told. Because while his intentions were to be fair and just, the truth was, he wasn't sure how he'd react if he had proof that Patrick was his. One thing was for sure, he wouldn't be able to stay away from his son.

Not a chance of that happening.

And that would almost certainly mean hurting Delaney.

Chapter Ten

Her cell phone rang, and Delaney cringed.

Her entire body seemed to be in some heightened state of anxiety. And that anxiety wasn't likely to go away anytime soon.

Especially considering the call was probably from the lab.

Ryan had had a courier pick up the test within a half hour of their nighttime chat. Well over twelve hours ago. In other words, plenty of time.

That meant Patrick's DNA results were perhaps already back.

Drawing in a deep breath, Delaney reached into her purse, took out her phone and stared down at the number on her caller ID.

"The lab?" Ryan asked. Obviously, he was experiencing some high anxiety, too.

"Probably. It's a local number."

Ryan didn't ask anything else. Instead, he chose to stare out the window of his limo, not that there was much to see. They were still minutes away from the New Hope clinic, and since his driver was the one taking them, staring out the window was probably the best defense Ryan could muster.

Trying to muster some defenses of her own, Delaney forced herself to answer the phone.

"Ms. Nash, it's Dr. Keyes," the caller said.

Okay. Not the call she'd dreaded but instead one she'd desperately wanted. Because she was certain that Keyes knew a lot more than he'd told her that rainy day in the parking lot.

"It's Keyes," she mouthed to Ryan.

He immediately moved closer. So close that their shoulders were touching. He put his ear next to the phone.

"Dr. Keyes," Delaney said, attempting to remain cordial. "A lot of people, including the police, have been trying to get in touch with you."

"It hasn't been a good time for me to talk to anyone."

I'll bet. But Delaney kept that remark to herself.

"My secretary said that Ryan McCall has an appointment with Dr. Montgomery." Keyes tossed that out as if he were testing the waters.

Delaney decided to test some waters of her own. "We're headed there now, to ask him some questions about what you and I discussed."

"That wouldn't be wise." No water testing that time. The words were brusquely delivered, and they sounded very much like a threat.

She glanced at Ryan, and his suddenly tight jaw confirmed that he thought it might be an attempt at intimidation. "Why wouldn't it be wise?" she asked.

"Because I think Emmett Montgomery might be behind everything that's happened. The cloning, the cover-up. Even Dr. Spears's missing records. Ms. Nash, has it occurred to you that you could be in danger?"

She almost laughed. "Yes, it's occurred to me." Still, it was an attention getter to hear it spelled out by the very man who might be the perpetrator.

Well, maybe.

There was still that whole angle with her father. Perhaps the fire and the car incident had nothing to do with the New Hope clinic. Maybe it was just a continuation of the bad blood between her father and Ryan. If so, this visit to Dr. Montgomery could be a waste of time.

But Delaney didn't believe that.

Even if Dr. Montgomery was innocent of the scare tactics—and she wasn't at all sure that he was—it didn't mean he hadn't known about or even approved the cloning experiments that resulted in Patrick's birth.

"Montgomery will try to shift the blame onto someone else," Keyes continued. "But don't make the mistake of thinking he's innocent. He's not. And if you believe him, if you trust him, it could be the last mistake you ever make."

That comment apparently reached Ryan's threshold for bullying and coercion. He snatched the phone from her. "Keyes, this is Ryan McCall. Cut the gaslight BS and start talking. I want to know exactly what happened at the New Hope clinic when you were Delaney's physician."

Delaney wanted to hear the response, and she shifted, moving closer to Ryan. But she soon learned there was no response to hear.

Keyes had hung up.

Ryan cursed. "Coward. But it doesn't matter," he said, handing her the phone. "We'll find him and get him to tell us what he knows."

"You think Keyes is responsible for the cloning—if there actually was a cloning, that is?"

Ryan turned to her. It seemed as if he were about to launch into an argument to convince her that the illegal procedure had indeed happened. But the argument faded. His face relaxed. "Keyes is covering up something. Or else he's scared and hiding. Either way, he knows something." And that was it. No declaration that he was positive Patrick was his son.

Maybe because he wasn't positive?

With all the agony Ryan had gone through with his wife and son's deaths perhaps he looked at her son and *wanted* Patrick to be Adam.

And maybe that was wishful thinking on her part.

"Are you sorry I ever told you about all of this?" she asked.

"Never." Ryan didn't look at her, but he did slip his hand over hers. A quiet, gentle gesture. It wasn't congruent with the intense expression on his face.

The driver stopped in the parking of the clinic. Delaney glanced at the single-story brownstone building, and she could feel her throat closing up. Yes, they might get answers from Dr. Montgomery, but it wasn't the answers that troubled her. It was dealing with what they would perhaps learn.

Just the night before, after their latest ill-advised kissing session, Ryan had promised her that he wouldn't try to take Patrick from her. While his promise had rid her of *some* of her fears, it didn't solve all their problems. There were several facets to this, and Delaney prayed there wouldn't be another attempt on their lives before they could sort through the situation.

Her throat was closing even tighter. She glanced at Ryan as they stepped from the limo. "Reassure me one more time that you have the best security available at your estate."

He nodded, slid his arm around her waist and moved them toward the clinic entrance. "Plus, there are two guards at the front gate. They have orders not to let anyone in while we're gone. I wouldn't take chances with Patrick's life. He's safe."

That helped.

So did his arm around her waist. Comforting and protecting. Something she'd learned Ryan was very good at it. Unfortunately, it could easily become a crutch. This relationship was temporary. It couldn't possibly be anything else since they were from different worlds. It would end as quickly as it had begun. And a month from now, she wouldn't even remember the taste of Ryan McCall.

Delaney actually stopped and let that thought sink in.

She had to admit that it was a sad time in a woman's life when she started lying to herself.

A month from now she would indeed remember Ryan. And that included his taste, his scent, his voice. Everything about him seemed permanently branded on her.

She groaned softly and gritted her teeth. "This is crazy," she whispered.

"Crazy." Not a question. More like an agreement. "You're thinking about this energy between us?"

Confused, surprised and slightly annoyed, she looked at him. "You have ESP?"

He shook his head, made a furtive glance around the parking lot and walked with her to the building. He stopped in the entry, just outside the receptionist's office. "But you've definitely been on my mind. I keep having these images of you in my head."

"Mercy, now there are images? Don't elaborate on them," Delaney insisted when he opened his mouth. "Trust me, I've got images in my head, too, and they're clear enough without you adding details."

"Is there kissing involved in your images?" He said it with a straight face. A straight, tortured face shadowed by frustration.

"Oh, yeah," she admitted. "How about your images?"

The torture increased and his groan matched hers. "Kisses, nudity, multiple orgasms."

She paused. Blinked. "Your images might be slightly better than mine."

He laughed, not from humor. It contained more frustration. He leaned in and brushed his mouth over hers. "Then, obviously that kiss last night didn't have the same effect on you as it did on me."

"I beg to differ. It had an effect. It's still having an effect." They stared at each other, and both mumbled some profanity at the same time. "I have a lot of reasons not to fall for you," she said.

"Ditto—"

"My father," Delaney continued. "The fact that he would see a relationship between us as a threat and would make our lives hell—"

"The fact that I'm not sure I can even let myself fall for you. The best I can offer is something temporary and physical, and the truth is, I don't even know if I can deliver in the physical area."

She furrowed her brow to show her skepticism.

"Okay, so I can deliver in that area," he amended. Probably because he remembered his physical reaction to her when they'd kissed.

Delaney certainly remembered it.

The heat rolled through her. Even now,

when there should be no heat. Only focus. Because they had a lot more important things to do than lust after each other.

"So what do we do?" she asked, trying to force that heat to cool. "How do we stop this?"

"Truth? I doubt we can stop it. I'd suggest we just go with it. Fall into bed and act out those fantasies. That way, we can get sweaty and hot and maybe try to burn out some of this fire."

"But?"

He shook his head. "But I keep thinking what happens afterward. Will you think I slept with you for some other reason other than to satisfy this need gnawing away at us? Will you hate me? Because, you see, Delaney, I can't have you going back to hating me."

Okay. That didn't sound, well, sexual. It sounded like more. Much more.

Didn't it?

And if so, how much more?

The possibilities both terrified her and tugged at her heartstrings. She seriously doubted she could go back to the way things were. Not after everything they'd been through. But heaven knew she needed some kind of protection, some way to guard her heart.

As did he.

Ryan had made it clear that he might never be free to love again, because of the risk. And she was a risk. The ultimate one since Delaney wasn't sure she could ever share Patrick with him.

And that was her reason for not responding, for not assuring him that she wouldn't hate him. It was a flimsy barrier, but a barrier all the same.

She checked her watch and started walking toward the receptionist area. "It's time for our appointment."

Ryan stopped her. He combed his gaze over her as if looking for answers.

Answers she couldn't give him.

"Let's talk to Montgomery," she insisted. "And then when we know what we're up against—"

"I'll still want you, Delaney."

She stared at him. "Yes, but why?"

Ryan didn't seem at all surprised by what would have been a vague question for anyone else. "You're thinking that I have the hots for you because of Patrick?"

Delaney nodded.

"Trust me, that's not why."

With that, he jerked open the door that separated them from the perky-looking blond receptionist.

"Ms. Nash," the woman greeted, obviously recognizing her.

Delaney probably should have recognized her too, but Ryan's comment had pretty much shot her focus. What was she going to do about this man by her side? A man who had her common sense and emotions turned upside down. Worse, she was beginning to think the condition wasn't temporary.

Or reversible.

"Ms. Nash?" the receptionist repeated.

Delaney glanced at the woman and realized she was standing stock-still at a time when inertia wasn't a good thing. She needed to move. To get this interview started with Montgomery. She didn't need other things, like her feelings about Ryan, to get in the way.

And that was true on so many levels.

"We're ready to see the doctor," Delaney insisted. She didn't dare look at Ryan.

"Come this way. He's expecting you."

The receptionist led them down a corridor. Since it wasn't a huge building, there were only four other offices off the hall, and the doctor's was at the end. He stood there, in the doorway, apparently waiting for them. Seeing him immediately focused her attention back on the reason for this visit.

Montgomery was tall, imposing, and looked more like an underwear model than a physician. His bulky arm and chest muscles strained the fabric of his white silk shirt. He was in his mid-thirties with sun-streaked brown hair and bronze-colored skin that probably hadn't come from a tanning bed but rather frequent trips to some tropical island.

Delaney had seen the man only a couple of times, during the months when she'd been Keyes's patient, but Dr. Montgomery shook her hand and greeted her as if they were old friends. A stark contrast to Keyes and his clandestine approach to avoiding the police. And her.

"Sit, please," the doctor offered, motioning toward two leather chairs across from his desk. "I have to admit I'm nervous about this visit—what with the recent accusations from the watchdog group."

"I can imagine. Are the accusations true?" Delaney asked, figuring the direct approach would save them time. She sat in one of the chairs; Ryan took the other.

"We provide fertility assistance to people who want children. We're not in the business of experimental research."

Despite the roundabout denial, Ryan zeroed right in on that. "So you won't mind providing us with the names of the couple who supplied the donor embryo for Delaney's son."

The doctor's amicable expression slipped a notch. "I can't do that. I'm sure you understand that I'm bound by confidentiality."

That was exactly what Delaney figured he'd say. It wouldn't stop her, though, from pressing. "But you're positive you used legitimate donors, and that Dr. Spears or someone else didn't get the embryo by some other means?"

"Positive, as far as my own actions are concerned." The doctor sighed, leaned back in his chair and tented his fingers. "Unfortunately, I can't guarantee that we didn't have a loose cannon in our midst."

"You mean the late Dr. Spears?" Ryan

questioned. Thankfully. Because it was something that definitely needed to be asked.

"Perhaps. Or maybe even Dr. Keyes. Keyes and a former employee who worked as a lab technician claim to have seen Spears's records, but I've found nothing to indicate that Spears was involved in anything questionable."

That was a start, but Delaney knew it was a tenuous one. After all, the assurance was coming from a man who'd perhaps tried to kill them.

"Maybe you've overlooked something," Ryan continued. "For instance, Spears's computer?"

Montgomery remained calm. "What about his computer?" he asked.

"It's missing. Or rather I should say both his home computer and the one he used here at work are nowhere to be found. For that matter, neither is Keyes or your former employee. In other words, both men who allegedly saw these illusive records have mysteriously disappeared."

Okay. That shot to pieces the tenuous assurance. While there might not be direct evidence to link Spears to the cloning, there appeared to be evidence of some suspicious activity, including a cover-up.

And if so, that would mean there was indeed something to cover up.

"Yes, the missing computers," Montgomery commented. "I don't know anything about Spears's personal computer, of course, but I'm looking into the one that was taken from here. I think maybe someone on the janitorial staff stole it. You just can't get good help these days. And as for the two men, Keyes just isn't very reliable. Neither is the lab tech. That's why he was fired." He calmly sipped some bottled water and recapped it. "But how is it that you have information about the computers?"

Ryan met the man's gaze. "My security manager looked into the matter."

She had to hand it to the doctor. He had little or no reaction to Ryan's statement. Which could mean he was totally innocent and all of this was just conversation about a late colleague. Or maybe Montgomery was simply very good at being deceptive.

"I also learned your clinic was located in the hospital where my son died," Ryan continued. "I know from phone records that Keyes, Spears and you were all working that afternoon. That would have given you or anyone else on your staff the opportunity to take DNA needed for experiments."

Montgomery took another long sip of water. "There'd be no reason for me to do such a thing. I have access to an ample supply of suitable embryos by equally suitable, *willing* donors."

Delaney moved to the edge of her seat. "But what if it's not about suitable supplies or willing donors? What if this is about something else?"

The doctor leaned closer, as well. He was near enough that Delaney could see the sweat forming on his upper lip. "So we're back to Keyes and his suspicious behavior. Then perhaps that's the direction your security manager and the police should be looking. I mean, he hasn't been at work in days, not since SAPD was here asking questions. If you ask me, those aren't the actions of an innocent man."

It was Ryan who finished her argument. "But as you pointed out, the clinic has enough embryos, so why would Dr. Keyes try to clone a child?"

"Hmm. Maybe he did it because he thought this would be the way to make medical history. A way to become famous."

"Don't you mean infamous?" Delaney challenged. "Human cloning is illegal."

"Yes, now it is. But laws change. Attitudes change. Maybe Dr. Keyes wanted to have the procedures and techniques perfected so that when it's legal, he would be a pioneer in the field."

A pioneer. Too bad her son might have been used to gain success for someone.

"I can think of another theory," Ryan calmly interjected. "As a businessman, I can see the financial benefits of such a project. Black-market cloning for people who perhaps want to replicate themselves for reasons of vanity. Or for those needing transplants. There are many who'd no doubt be willing to pay a fortune to have a second chance at life."

Oh, God. Suddenly she felt sick. Delaney had to press her fingers to her mouth. She fought to stay calm because now was not the time to lose her composure.

Montgomery nodded. "As in your situation, Mr. McCall. With the son that you lost. Um. Yes. I see your point. This could have been a highly profitable endeavor for Dr. Keyes."

"Or for you," Delaney pointed out.

The glare that Montgomery aimed at her contained none of the friendliness that the man had shown when they'd first arrived. "It's that sort of comment that makes the authorities open investigations."

Ryan started to speak, but Delaney gripped his arm, an indication that this was a battle she wanted to fight. "The police don't conduct investigations unless there's a reason for them to do so. I believe there's a good reason in this case."

"Are you saying you think I'm guilty?" Montgomery demanded.

"I'm saying you have as much motive and opportunity as Keyes."

Her accusation brought the doctor to his feet. Ryan stood, as well. No touch on his arm would have gotten him to back off. He pulled one of his knight routines and maneuvered himself between Montgomery and her.

"If Ms. Nash repeats what she just said

to anyone," the doctor warned, aiming an accusing finger in her direction, "I'll sue her for slander."

"I'm pretty good at countersuing," Ryan pointed out.

Since an argument probably wouldn't help get them those much-needed answers, Delaney stepped around Ryan so she could face the doctor.

"Lawsuits aside, I *will* learn the truth," she said. "And if you're involved, I'll make sure the authorities do everything to put you behind bars."

Montgomery's mouth tightened and his eyes narrowed. But what he didn't do was provide her with any more information. He went toward the door.

"You can see yourselves out," he said from over his shoulder.

And he was gone, slamming the door behind him.

Delaney considered going after him, but she doubted that would accomplish anything other than provide the fodder for Montgomery to get a restraining order against her.

"Either he or Keyes could have assisted Spears with the experiments," Ryan said, leading her out of the office. They retraced their steps down the hall and went out the front door. "Or both."

Yes. In fact, a collaboration would make sense. After all, all three men worked in the clinic. All three apparently stood to gain a lot, financially, from it. "Except we're right back where we started."

"Not quite. We shook things up today. If Montgomery is guilty, he might do something stupid to cover his tracks. If that's the case, my security manager might be able to get some proof."

Delaney glanced around the parking lot as they approached the waiting limo. "Your security manager's here?"

"He's around. He'll be watching Montgomery over the next few days."

Days. For some reason, that sounded like an eternity. "I don't think my body can stand all this high-level anxiety much longer. Eventually, I'll crash and burn."

The crash and burn had some significant fuel added to it when her phone rang again. Delaney waited until she and Ryan were inside the limo before she glanced down at the screen. A local number. And not the one that had appeared when Keyes had called earlier.

"Hello," she answered. Beside her, Ryan stilled. She couldn't even hear him breathing. The only sound came from the driver as he pulled out of the parking lot and started back toward the estate.

"Ms. Nash?"

Not Keyes. But a woman. "Yes?"

"I'm Sarah Cantrell, from the lab. I compared your son's DNA to Mr. McCall's, and I have the results."

Delaney felt her stomach clench, as did her heart. "Okay." It was all she could manage to say.

"Uh, if you'd prefer," the woman added, obviously noting Delaney's hesitance. "I can have a courier deliver the information to you."

It was tempting. But even though it might be slightly easier to get the results while she was alone, Delaney knew it would only delay the inevitable. "No. You can tell me now."

"Okay. Well, I need to let you know up front that the test is ninety-nine-point-nine-nine-nine percent accurate so there's little chance of error. However, if you want it repeated—"

"I don't. I just want the results."

"All right. I compared Patrick Nash's DNA to that of the other subject, Ryan McCall. And I can say with certainty that Mr. McCall is the biological father of your son."

Chapter Eleven

Ryan waited.

Every nerve in his body was on alert. Not in a good way. But in a way that made him think of panic attacks and nausea.

He watched as Delaney pressed the end call button on her phone and slipped it back into her purse. She gave away nothing. Yes, there was emotion practically burning in her eyes, and her bottom lip was trembling. She almost immediately started to twist her butterfly-less ring. Still, he didn't know if it was because the test results had been negative or positive.

He waited some more.

Waited, while Delaney tried to steady her breathing. While she clamped her teeth over her bottom lip. While she glanced at everything in the limo but him.

"Patrick is your son." Delaney said the words fast. As if she were afraid if she didn't, she might not be able to get it all out.

The impact hit Ryan just as quickly. Oh, man. It was an onslaught of too many emotions to identify, and it made him thankful he was sitting down. Those emotions tore through his head as the scenery raced past the windows of the limo. Taking him home.

"Home to my son," Ryan mumbled.

It was all he could say. He looked down at his body to see if he was shaking. Surprisingly, he wasn't. From all outward appearances, he was calm. But inside, well, that was an entirely different story. There was nothing calm about the maelstrom of emotion he was experiencing.

His son was alive.

Adam was alive.

All those hours, those days, those endless nights that he'd tried to bargain with God to give him back his wife and son. And God had apparently bargained with him after all. He'd been given back his little boy. A second chance.

A miracle.

Ironic. Because his miracle was possibly someone else's felony.

And the onset of Delaney's own personal nightmare.

That was a much-needed nudge back to reality, and Ryan looked at her. Her face said it all. What she was experiencing was the antithesis of what he was. She was scared. And she probably thought she was on the verge of losing everything. Another irony, since Ryan felt as if he'd been given back his life.

The joy of regaining his life stayed with him.

For another moment or two.

Until he remembered the danger.

Until he remembered the fire and the car accident with Delaney. Someone obviously wanted to hurt or even kill them. That possibly included Patrick. And in the blink of an eye, he could end up losing everything all over again.

That was the problem with being given back his life.

If he lost it again, if he lost Patrick, there wasn't a chance he could recover a second time.

"Say something," Delaney begged. "*Any-*

thing. Lie if you have to, but tell me that everything's going to be all right."

Ryan couldn't promise her that, and he was afraid a lie would stick in his throat. Besides, this was Delaney, and she deserved better than a lie. What she deserved was the truth.

If only he knew what the truth was.

"A lot of clichés come to mind, Delaney. Clichés about not being able to undo the past. It's time to move forward. But to you, all of that must sound like BS."

"Scary BS." She turned. "Remember when I told you how my parents fought for custody of me? Well, it was bad. *Very* bad. I can't put Patrick through that."

The sheer emotion in her voice made him ache for her. "It doesn't have to be that way."

"Doesn't it?" she snapped. "He's your son. You'll want to raise him. Maybe you don't feel that way right now because you're trying to consider my feelings. But you *will* want to raise him."

Ryan didn't contradict her. "He's your son, too. You carried him for nine months, gave birth to him. You've nursed him every day of his life. You love him."

She dismissed him with a shake of her head. "And all of that can be negated with the results from that DNA test and a trip to a good custody lawyer. Patrick is biologically your son. Legally—"

"No. We're not going there." He took her shoulders and forced her to face him. "No lawyers. No custody hearings. Just us."

She stared at him. "What does that mean?"

"It means we work this out, together. Somehow." Unfortunately, it was the *somehow* that was giving Ryan a few problems.

"And we're back to shared custody. No. I won't go through that."

"So you've said." He glanced out the window as the driver went through the gates of the estate. He was mere minutes from being inside. "Tell you what, let's table this discussion. Because my brain is thinking of only one thing—seeing Patrick—and I can't work out details. Just rest assured that we will work them out."

Delaney cooperated. Maybe because she didn't have a choice. With a terrified look on her face, she sat silently, waiting, for the driver to come to a stop in front of the house. Ryan tried not to rush out, tried not to break into a run, but it took every ounce of willpower to calmly get out and follow Delaney into the foyer.

"Go on to the nursery," she said. "I'll give you a few minutes alone with him."

It was a gift. A truly selfless one. One that had cost her, and Ryan knew exactly how high that cost was. "You're an amazing woman."

She turned away from him, probably so he wouldn't see the tears in her eyes. Ryan noted them anyway. And he hated that this was breaking her heart.

"Go," she insisted when he reached for her. "We'll talk later."

She even gave him a little push in the direction of the stairs. Ryan hesitated, wondering if he should try to do something about those tears, but he couldn't wait any longer. He had to see his son.

He wasn't sure how he made it up the stairs. Each step seemed to take an eternity, and yet it felt as if he were flying. He tried to rein in his heart, to hold back if only a little, but he soon realized that wasn't possible.

Ryan went through the door of the nursery. Lena was there, and she had Patrick in her lap. The child turned his head in Ryan's direction and doled out one of those priceless smiles.

Lena stood, obviously sensing something. "Boss, are you all right?"

"I am now."

Ryan forced his feet to move, and he went to his son. He reached down for him before he remembered that he'd never held a four-month-old child. He took the cue from Lena, and Ryan slid his hand around Patrick, to support his back and neck, and drew his son to him.

The pain of the past two years seemed to melt away.

Oh, man.

He'd expected something powerful, something that he would remember forever. And it was. But even that was an understatement. At the moment, miracles themselves were an understatement because this was the miracle to beat them all.

"Are you all right?" Lena repeated.

Ryan nodded, not taking his attention away from the child he held in his arms.

Patrick eyed him with intense curiosity and finally reached out. His tiny fingers made an awkward pass at Ryan's chin, swiping it. Patrick made a few more attempts, his aim obviously not perfect yet, and he managed to grab Ryan's nose.

Patrick laughed. A cheerful hiccupping sound that lit up his whole face.

Another miracle.

Ryan caught some movement out of the corner of his eye and turned defensively toward it. However, there was no threat.

It was Delaney.

The tears that had been in her eyes while she was downstairs were now streaming down her cheeks. Those tears and her expression said it all. The grief. The fear.

And the hurt.

Before he could say anything, she turned and hurried out of the room.

DELANEY PRACTICALLY SPRINTED into the bedroom of her guest suite and snatched up her purse. She wanted nothing more than to grab Patrick and run. To leave the estate and put some miles between Ryan and them.

That was her first reaction. Her own version of fight or flight, with the flight option definitely winning out. But slowly it sank in that fleeing wasn't a good idea. She couldn't react out of emotion, and yet she seemed to have no choice about it.

Feeling as if her heart were about to break apart, Delaney dropped down onto the edge of the bed and tried to choke back the tears.

She failed.

Disgusted with herself, she slapped her hand on the mattress. Before this past week, crying, for her, had been a semiannual event limited to days with really bad PMS or occasional breakups with boyfriends. But she'd cried buckets since she learned about the cloning allegations. And it sobered her to admit that there would probably be a lot more tears before this was over.

"If you punch me instead of the mattress, it might help," she heard Ryan say.

She blinked away enough tears to see him standing in the doorway.

Alone.

"Where's Patrick?" she asked, alarmed.

"Lena has him. He's fine." He tipped his head to the purse she still clutched in her hand. "Are you looking for the fastest escape route?"

"No. I was a few minutes ago, but I decided that it would be stupid to run." She stood, took a deep breath and tried to steady herself. "Still, a drive might do me some good, and I do need to pick up papers from my house."

Ryan ambled closer. "Is that the truth?"

"Yes." She considered it, decided it was indeed the truth, and provided him with another *yes*. "But I really do need to get some work done. And I won't run. I promise. But don't expect me to just hand my son over to you. *Your* son," she corrected.

"Try *our* son. It might be the compromise you're looking for."

"This isn't some business deal—"

"No." Unlike her voice, his was calm. "It's far more important than that." He stopped in front of her and reached out. Ryan took her by the shoulders and pulled her into his arms.

Because she didn't want to be comforted, because she *couldn't* be comforted, Delaney pushed him away. Turned. To head for Patrick's room. But she only made it a couple of steps before Ryan reached her.

He whirled her around to face him.

The emotion caught up with her, too, and Delaney knew she was on the verge of an all-out crying session or perhaps even a temper tantrum. She didn't want to have either in front of Ryan.

"I'm calling a bodyguard service," she said, knowing she wasn't thinking this through. "Then, I'm leaving."

"You're not," he countered.

Mercy, that riled her. Not a mild riling, either. How dare he tell her that she couldn't leave. Wasn't it enough that she was losing her son to him. Did she have to take orders from him, too?

Delaney threw off his grip with far more force than required and stormed toward the nursery. Ryan cut her off at the pass so to speak. He hooked his arm around her waist, turned, and their forward momentum sent them against the nursery door, shutting it.

Ryan took the brunt of the impact, his back landing hard against the door. "I don't want to argue with you."

"Tough." Delaney geared up to deliver something scathing. Something born of the fear and the anger she was feeling.

Something she'd no doubt regret saying but intended to anyway.

However, intentions were as far as she got.

Ryan pulled her closer until he had her in a snug embrace. "I just need to feel you in my arms right now."

It wasn't some sexual suggestion but more of a heart-wrenching confession, and she didn't think it was her imagination that it was a confession he hadn't wanted to make.

Delaney knew for a fact it wasn't a confession she wanted to hear.

She shook her head. Not because she didn't want him to hold her. Heaven help her, she did.

But she didn't stay tucked in his embrace.

In fact, because of the fear and all the uncertainty, she moved away from him.

And Ryan let her go.

He stood there, with his back against the nursery door. She could read every emotion on his face. Nothing hidden. This wasn't the ruthless businessman but someone who was experiencing all the pain and joy of the news they'd just learned. His son was alive.

Maybe it was because he didn't reach for her. Or maybe it was because she, too, needed to hold him. Whatever the reason, Delaney retraced her steps.

Ryan's eyes met hers. He started to say something, but because there was still some of the questioning and the argument in the depths of his blue eyes, she pressed her fingertips to his mouth. She was so close that she had the pleasure of seeing his pulse jump in his throat.

Her own pulse did the same.

She reached out and pulled him to her.

They could ruin everything for each other by squabbling over custody, by letting the past stop them from trying to work out a future.

It felt right to hold him.

To be held.

She melted into his arms.

They stood there for long moments. With his heartbeat drumming against hers. His uneven breath on her face. And they simply held each other.

"Before you came here, there weren't a lot of good memories in this house," he said. "With Sandra and my son's deaths.

Plus, the time I spent here as child was some of the worst of my life."

Delaney didn't know what to say; instead she listened.

"Uncle Jess didn't want me here," Ryan continued. "So he just ignored me. Never made eye contact. Never acknowledged me, even if we were in the same room."

She could see it. Ryan, as a ten-year-old. An outsider. A lost child. Unloved. Unwanted. No wonder it was so important to him to create his own family.

And that family now almost certainly included Patrick.

"Thank you," Ryan whispered.

"For what?" Delaney had to speak around the lump in her throat.

"For just being here. For acknowledging me. For this."

Oh, how his words touched her heart and made her ache for the childhood he'd never had.

Part of her wanted their embrace, this moment, to last forever, but from the other room, she heard her son fussing. An indication that *forever* was about to come to an end.

"It's time for me to nurse him," she remembered, checking her watch. Delaney hadn't needed that glance though. Patrick's fussy cry and her own breasts let her know that it was time.

She and Ryan pulled away from each other, both reacting very much like parents, putting their child first.

The sunlight filtering through the window flickered over them. Over Ryan. And some of the rays landed on his etched wedding band. A glint of gold danced over her.

She could have sworn her heart stopped beating.

Noticing his ring was nothing out of the ordinary. She'd seen it dozens of times, but for now it was like a revelation. Ryan couldn't be anything less than a father to his son. She couldn't be anything less than a mother.

That, however, didn't give them a basis to be together.

While Delaney didn't want a split-custody arrangement, nor did she want a loveless relationship. And whether Ryan wanted to admit it or not, he was still married. To Sandra. He still wore his wedding ring, a symbol of their love.

Of course, Ryan would welcome her

into his life, maybe even into some small part of his heart. For Patrick's sake. Maybe even for his.

But Delaney now understood that he couldn't give her himself.

That's why she had to put a lock on own heart. To put some emotional distance between Ryan and her. Because while his arms made her feel as if he were hers, he wasn't.

And he never would be.

Chapter Twelve

Grumbling about what he'd just learned from the call to his security manager, Ryan went in search of Delaney. He found her exactly where he figured she'd be. She was still in the nursery, holding Patrick, though the baby was no longer nursing. He'd fallen asleep in her arms.

It was a peaceful scene, not exactly congruent with the thoughts about that call. Or the rather tumultuous encounter they'd had in her bedroom. Still, Ryan took a moment to savor it.

Delaney had her attention focused on Patrick. She was rocking him, softly humming. Patrick was settled into the crook of her arm, and even though her left breast was still exposed and ready for him to continue nursing, Patrick was zonked out.

The moment Delaney spotted him, she pulled her top back in place, eased out of the rocking chair and settled the baby in his crib. It was a routine she probably went through four, five times a day, but it was far from routine for Ryan. He would never take it for granted that he'd been given another chance to be a father.

Touching her finger to her lips in a *shh* gesture, Delaney walked past him and into her suite. Even though she was a little aloof, all right she was a lot aloof—Ryan didn't become overly concerned until she picked up her purse.

"I've already called my day care manager to tell her that I won't be coming in to work for a while, but I need to go to my house and pick up the payroll checks for my employees. I have to sign them, or they won't get paid. Will your driver be able take me?" she asked. Her request was more as if she were informing him of a decision she'd already made.

"Of course." Ryan used the intercom on the wall to buzz Lena. "Have a car and driver brought to the front. And I need you to watch Patrick. Ms. Nash and I have to make a quick trip into San Antonio."

"Sure, boss."

Delaney made a slight huffing sound, but she didn't say anything until he clicked off the intercom. "The reason I asked to use your driver was so you can stay here with Patrick."

It was tempting.

But it was a bad idea.

"I'm coming with you," Ryan said, and he followed Delaney out of the door and into the hall.

She glanced over her shoulder as she made her way down the stairs. She frowned and walked faster. "This isn't necessary. I'm sure your driver will play body-guard for an hour or so, and you no doubt have more important things to do."

He had work, yes, but it wasn't as important as going with her.

"Do I have to remind you what happened the last time we were at your house?" Ryan glanced up at the sky when they went outside. It was cloudy in a way that could indicate another spring storm was on the way. No storm would stop him today.

Once they were under the portico, Ryan opened the door of the limo for her, and when she just stared at him, he motioned for her to get inside. "Save your breath," Ryan insisted. "I'm going with you."

After what he'd just learned from Quentin, that wasn't up for negotiation.

Because Delaney seemed in a rotten mood, he expected her to continue the argument, but she didn't. She mumbled a thank-you and settled in the seat next to him.

Close enough that he could have nudged her leg with his.

And yet, it wasn't very close at all.

Something had happened since their last encounter in her bedroom. Something that had put the old walls back up between them. Ryan couldn't let those walls stay, of course. Because for better or worse, they were on the same side.

Now, he had to convince Delaney of that.

"I talked to Quentin," Ryan said. He waited, letting his hesitation prepare her for news she wasn't going to like. Ryan didn't care much for it, either. "He's had P.I.s watching both of our *friends*—your father and Emmett Montgomery. However, your former doctor, Bryson Keyes, has been elusive. Quentin hasn't been able to find him yet."

They drove through the gate, and she studied the two guards inside the gatehouse. "And?"

"And we're still no closer to eliminating one of them as a suspect in either the fire or the car incident."

She stayed quiet a moment, most likely absorbing what he was saying. "What about alibis?"

"They don't have any. Well, at least none that can be verified. Plus, your father's been driving near the estate. Not actually on the grounds, of course. The guards wouldn't dare let him in, but yesterday he was on this road. The P.I. was ready to call the sheriff when your father made a U-turn and headed back to San Antonio."

"Oh, mercy." She blew out a long breath. "The incidents might not be related to what went on at New Hope clinic."

"We don't know that. Keyes is nowhere to be found, and Montgomery hasn't left his house since we visited him at the clinic. Sounds like the actions of two guilty men if you ask me."

She shook her head and shoved her hands into her hair. "I want this to be over."

"It will be."

"Will it?" she snapped. "Someone wants to hurt us, Ryan. Maybe worse. Maybe someone even wants us dead, and it isn't comforting to know that *someone* might be my own father."

He could see her point. But then, he'd seen that point for a while since he'd been on the receiving end of Nash's threats and antics. "Have you thought about having him committed to an institution?"

"Lately, yes! And if he's behind this, I'll have him put away. Because I've felt guilty about not saving his business, I've let him get by with things. But not anymore. I'm done with this whole guilt-riddled-daughter routine. I did everything I could to save his business. *Everything.*"

There it was. Spelled out for him. Ryan had always considered what all of this had done to Nash, but it had obviously affected Delaney, too. "And I did everything to take it away from him."

She waved him off. "I didn't tell you how I felt to transfer my guilt to you. Besides, you were just being you."

"Ouch."

"Sorry." She closed her eyes a moment. "Maybe I should have said it was you just dealing with your grief the only way you knew how—by throwing yourself into your work."

Yes, but in the past few days, work hadn't sated him the way it used to. Of course, lately he'd felt very needy. That didn't go with his iceman image. But then, that image was changing.

Delaney and his son were responsible for that.

"Now, as for Patrick," Ryan said. He didn't give her a chance to object to the abrupt change of subject. "We have some options. *You* have some options. The most logical one is for Patrick and you to stay at the estate indefinitely."

She angled toward him, and examined him. "I have a house, thank you. And the estate is your home, not ours."

"But it could be."

More body angling. More examination. She frowned. "Think this through, Ryan. What will your family and your business associates think if Patrick and I move in with you?"

He shrugged. "Not a problem. I don't care what my associates think. And other than a few distant cousins, I have no family."

Except for Patrick.

And it was because of Patrick that Ryan had come up with the next option. A risky one. He hoped Delaney didn't demand to get out of the car when she heard it. They were driving past the drainage ditch where the incident had occurred, and he didn't want to be in the vicinity any longer than necessary.

"We could look at this from a different angle," Ryan offered. "One that could solve our dilemma about Patrick and your other concerns."

"What angle?" Delaney asked, her tone skeptical.

Since Ryan didn't think he stood a chance of making it sound agreeable, he just laid it there and hoped for the best. "You could marry me."

DELANEY WAITED for Ryan to break into laughter at his joke. But after several snail-crawling moments, there was no laughter, and it became clear that he hadn't intended for it to be humorous.

"Marry you?" she questioned.

Ryan nodded. "It makes sense. No shared custody because we'd be in a committed relationship under the same roof. Both of us would be able to raise Patrick."

She glanced in the mirror and saw the driver, Clancy. The elderly man with the sugar-white hair and time-etched face was staring at them with almost parental concern. Ryan obviously noticed it, too, and tossed him a scowl.

Clancy quickly looked away.

Delaney debated several things she could say in response to Ryan's suggestion, but instead she took his hand, lifted it, so that his wedding ring was right in front of his eyes. "You're already married."

Ryan looked at the ring as if seeing it for the first time. He cursed and shook his head. "I should have taken it off months ago."

"You obviously weren't ready to do that. Besides, I won't say *I do* to resolve our custody issues. I don't take marriage vows lightly."

He pulled back his shoulders, looking genuinely offended. "Neither do I. But this isn't just about us. We've got to consider what's best for Patrick. Plus, it's not as if we hate each other—right?" He waited a moment. "Right?" he repeated when she didn't answer.

"I don't hate you." It was the truth. Well, partly.

She didn't hate him.

And it was entirely possible she was falling in love with him.

Still, that and that alone wasn't the basis for a marriage. Especially when the love was one-sided.

He reached for his ring, a motion that indicated he was about to yank it from his finger. Delaney clamped her hand over his and stopped him. "Don't do this. Wait until you're ready."

"I'm ready." But the grief in his eyes, a grief she couldn't reach, couldn't touch, was still there. And she had to accept that it might always be there.

"You're not," she insisted.

Ryan moved her hand away. "Delaney, I wouldn't have kissed you if I hadn't thought there was a chance that it would lead to a permanent relationship between us."

She frowned and stared at him, not believing what he was saying.

"Okay, I would have kissed you," he amended, flexing his eyebrows. "I'm a man. Blame it on testosterone and the way I feel when I look at you."

She met his gaze head-on. "I'm not Sandra."

"And I don't want you to be. I loved her. Truly loved her. But that doesn't mean there isn't room in my heart for you."

It was a step. A huge one. However, it wasn't enough. "You don't love me, Ryan."

Silence.

The kind of silence accompanied by a deer-caught-in-the-headlight look.

"Don't worry," she assured him so she could end the uncomfortable silence. "I don't expect you to lie and say you feel something for me that you don't. I just want you to see that marriage isn't an option."

Even if part of her wanted it to be.

Imagine—marriage to Ryan McCall? A week ago, Delaney would have considered it unthinkable, and now it seemed to take hold of her.

Ryan's wife.

His lover.

The two of them raising Patrick together.

Her, waking up to him each morning. And, yes, maybe even him falling in love with her. But that was a slippery fantasy that could easily go another direction, and she could end up with a broken heart. Ryan might never learn to love her, might never be able to let go of the past.

Disgusted with herself and her reaction to Ryan's proposal, Delaney borrowed a trick from him and stared out the window. Not that she actually saw the scenery. No. Her mind and every other part of her were on his proposal.

She'd rejected it. Adamantly. But perhaps she shouldn't have. Marriage with love was the ideal, but for the sake of her son perhaps she could bring her ideal goals down to a more realistic level.

She glanced at Ryan.

She'd come to know him quite well in a short period of time. Delaney could thank the danger and Patrick's circumstances for that. But it didn't change what she felt in the deepest part of her heart. She couldn't marry a man who didn't love her. That would set her up to relive her parents' mistake of trying to be together for the sake of a child.

"What the hell?" she heard Ryan mumble.

Delaney followed his gaze out his own window and spotted a glint of...something. Something in the thick cluster of trees about twenty yards from the road. She didn't even have time to speculate about what it was or why it had alarmed Ryan.

"Get down!" he yelled.

But he didn't wait for her to do that. Ryan dove at her, tackling her, and knocked her flat onto the seat.

She soon realized why he'd done that.

There was a shrill scream of sound. A horrible noise. Of metal ripping through the metal of the car. And the glass. Ryan's window shattered, the sheet of safety glass didn't spew toward them but instead crashed with a walloping thud onto them and the seat.

Ryan cursed, and she felt him fumbling in his jacket. For his gun, she realized. Worse, the driver slammed on his brakes. Stopping.

Delaney's breath froze. "Someone's

shooting at us?" she asked. Not a calm request for information, either. She practically shouted it. And a split-second later, she got her own confirmation.

Another blast.

Then another.

The bullets tore through the car, one gashing the roof, and the other slamming into the leather seat just an inch or so above Ryan's head.

It took ten years off her life to see how close the bullet had come. Delaney grabbed him and pulled hard, dragging him onto the floor with her.

"Clancy, get us out of here!" Ryan yelled to the driver.

The man groaned in pain. "I've been hit."

"Bad?" Ryan asked.

"Bad," the man confirmed.

Oh, God.

It was obvious the shooting wasn't just a scare tactic. No. This was real, and with each bullet, one of them could be killed.

Or maybe the damage had already been done.

Anger and adrenaline surged through her. It didn't matter if the shooter was her father, one of the doctors from New Hope or even someone else. The person was a would-be killer, and if she made it out of this alive, she would make sure he was stopped.

With his weapon in his hand, Ryan popped up long enough to look over the seat at the driver. He cursed and dropped back down. They made eye contact, and Delaney immediately saw all the emotion, all the anger, all the concern that was no doubt in her own eyes.

"It doesn't look good," Ryan informed her in a hoarse whisper.

Ryan moved, ready to come up so he could fire. Only then did Delaney realize what a huge risk that would be.

"No!" she shouted over the shots.

But Ryan ignored her. Bracing his right wrist with his left hand, he made use of the gaping hole where the window had once been, double-tapped the trigger of his gun, and shot toward the trees where she'd seen the glint of metal.

"I won't just sit here and let him kill us," Ryan informed her.

And with that, he came up again and fired another shot.

Delaney caught him when he came back down, and she was on the verge of telling him that she couldn't let him sacrifice his life. But then, she thought of Clancy, and she knew both she and Ryan would have to take some serious risks for all three of them to get out of this alive.

From the front seat, Clancy groaned again, and she heard a thump as if he'd collapsed onto the seat. Immediately, the car started to inch forward. The man had probably lost consciousness, causing his foot to come off the brake.

"You return fire," she told Ryan. "I'll see to Clancy."

Ryan grabbed her, probably to stop her, but Delaney had no intention of just letting the driver bleed or allowing the car to go off the road. Especially since the gunman could keep them pinned there indefinitely.

"I need to do this," she said to Ryan.

He looked ready to argue, but Delaney shook her head, indicating that this wasn't the time for a debate. Each second was vital if they hoped to keep Clancy alive.

Ryan nodded, finally. "Be careful," he warned, and he pressed a kiss on her cheek.

She mentally counted to three and levered herself over the seat. The first thing she saw was blood and lots of it. The man had been wounded in his left shoulder.

Delaney maneuvered her body around Clancy, dropped to the floor so she'd be out of the line of fire and jammed her hand on the brake. Reaching up, she managed to put the car into Park. That was one problem solved—they wouldn't end up in the ditch—but she was left with what to do about Clancy. Because of the day-care center, she had basic first-aid training. Hardly adequate for such a serious injury. And there was no doubt in her mind that this was serious.

She used her left hand to apply pressure to the wound, and while staying down, she used the car's mobile phone to call 911. She figured they could get out of there and meet the ambulance along the way. It would save them precious time. The emergency operator assured her that she would send the police and an ambulance immediately.

Unfortunately, immediately might not be soon enough.

"Everything will be all right, Clancy,"

she promised. But Delaney had no idea if that were true.

If it would *ever* be true.

If they made it out of this alive, and that was a big *if,* this might not be the last attempt. The gunman would likely continue until they stopped him or until he managed to kill them.

She ached at the thought. At the thought of losing Ryan. Sweet heaven. How had he become such an important part of her life, and her heart, in such a short period of time?

"Ryan, please tell me you're okay," Delaney called out.

He fired another round before he answered her. "Stay down!"

Since that lack of reassurance only made her stomach clench tighter, she nearly risked looking over the seat to check on him.

Then the shots stopped.

Delaney lay there, part of her body on the floor and the other on the seat. Listening. Waiting. Praying. For what seemed an eternity.

The silence settled in around them.

"He quit firing," she mumbled.

"Maybe," was Ryan's whispered response.

But the *maybe* began to look better and better when the moments slipped by.

"How's Clancy?" Ryan asked.

Delaney glanced down at the man. He was pasty-white and clearly in pain, but the pressure she was applying to the wound had slowed down the blood flow. Still, he needed medical attention. "The ambulance should be here soon."

She hoped.

Delaney eased Clancy away from the steering wheel so she could get behind it. Thankfully, he wasn't a heavy man, but during those precious seconds, she couldn't apply pressure to his wound, and he started to bleed again. She hurried. She threw the car into gear and stomped on the accelerator. The instant she had the car moving, she clamped her right hand back over his wound.

No gunshots.

No sign of the shooter at all.

Keeping as low in the seat as she could, Delaney glanced in the rearview mirror and spotted Ryan. All his attention was pinpointed to that window. His gun, aimed. Ready to fire. In fact, his entire body was tense and ready. He stayed that way until she reached the intersection that would take them to the main highway.

Still keeping his gun in position, he took out his phone and stabbed in some numbers.

"Quentin," she heard him say, "someone just shot at us. Clancy's hurt, and we're headed to the hospital. Make sure the guards are in place at the gate and the estate is secure. No one gets in, understand? *No one.*"

Delaney hadn't thought the knot in her stomach could get any tighter, or that her heart could pound any harder.

She was wrong.

"Patrick," she said on a rise of breath. With the distraction of the shooting, she hadn't thought about Patrick possibly being in danger.

"Alerting Quentin and the guards is just a precaution," Ryan assured her, meeting her eyes again in the mirror.

But it felt like more than a precaution.

A lot more.

Her baby was in danger.

"Pull every P.I. you have from their stations and get them to the estate ASAP," Ryan continued. "Call SAPD and Sheriff Knight. Let them know what's happened." And with that, he paused, apparently waiting for Quentin to comply. "They're on the way," he relayed to Delaney.

Ryan paused again. "Hell," he snarled a moment later. "When?"

That, coupled with the alarmed look on Ryan's face shot her adrenaline through the roof. Whatever Quentin had said to Ryan, it had upset him.

"Is it Patrick?" Delaney asked. She was already praying. Her son had to be all right.

"Patrick's fine," Ryan assured her. He ended the call, and she heard him pull in a hard breath. "Someone leaked the cloning allegations to the press. And they named names. *Our names.*"

Delaney shook her head. "Who would have leaked something like that?"

"The watchdog group, maybe. Or maybe it was Keyes or Montgomery. Maybe even the missing lab tech, Noel Kendall. He's in hiding, but that doesn't mean he wouldn't make a phone call to a reporter."

Because she'd feared much worse news, the leak didn't seem like such a dreadful thing.

Until it sank in.

"How and when did the leak happen?" Delaney wanted to know.

"This morning. It was in the *San Antonio Express-News*."

In other words, hours ago. Plenty of time for her father to read it.

And react.

Her father could have been the gunman hiding behind those trees. A cowardly act that could have left all three of them dead.

But Ryan was right. This didn't rule out the two doctors. After all, one could have leaked the info; the other could have decided to do something about it.

Stunned and angry, and getting angrier with each passing moment, Delaney focused on the road ahead. On the drive. Once Clancy was in the ambulance, she was going to the police and insist they bring her father in for questioning.

And, by God, the man better have answers.

Chapter Thirteen

Ryan had just finished his phone conversation with Quentin when he heard the sound. Not the rain, even though outside there were the rumblings of a storm moving in.

What he heard was a welcome sound, one he desperately needed to soothe some of the anger and fear that was building inside him right along with the storm.

He made his way from his office to the open doorway of the nursery and stood quietly while he watched Delaney and Patrick. Both were on a quilt on the floor. Patrick, on his back. Delaney, on her side. She was playing Little Piggy with his toes, and Patrick was giggling. Even though thick clouds hid the moon and the room was dimly lit, the sounds of their laughter filled the air with warmth and light. And the warmth and light made it all the way to Ryan's heart.

It was a feeling he wouldn't take for granted.

Earlier, he'd glanced at the security monitor while he made his calls, and he'd seen Delaney dressing Patrick after his bath. Now, his son was wearing one-piece pj's, decorated with frogs and ducks, and he smelled like baby powder.

Delaney's scent was there, too. Her shampoo from the shower she'd taken after they returned from the police station. He could smell her soap. Something tropical that she'd used to wash the blood off her.

Clancy's blood.

It could have just as easily been hers.

He'd nearly lost her today. *Again.* In this case three times was definitely not a charm. The ditch. The fire. The shooting. Ryan was willing to bet his right arm that the same person was responsible for all three attempts. Sloppy execution of equally sloppy and risky plans.

Yet, each one had come damn close to succeeding.

Sometimes a person didn't have to be good to succeed. Just lucky.

Smiling, still gently wiggling Patrick's toes, Delaney leaned over and kissed the baby's cheek. Patrick yawned and rubbed his eyes.

Ryan savored the scene in front of him for several moments before he stepped inside, knowing it would put a halt to the play. And it did. Delaney's head whipped in his direction, the questions were all over her face.

"How's Clancy?" Her whispered voice didn't mask the concern. No way. It was there, as it had been on her face and in her voice all afternoon. Ryan didn't expect it to go away anytime soon.

"He's stable. The doctors say he's going to be fine, but he'll have to stay in the hospital a few days. He's already complaining about the food. A good sign."

The relief she felt was all over her face. "What about your call to Sheriff Knight?"

Because Ryan wasn't totally ready to let go of the Little Piggy moment, he eased down onto the floor next to them. Patrick turned in his direction.

"The police still haven't located Dr. Keyes," Ryan explained. While the topic of conversation was definitely serious, he tried to smile so he wouldn't alarm his son. "And the P.I.s who were watching your father and Dr. Montgomery say neither man left his residence."

"They could have slipped out."

"Absolutely. And that's why SAPD is questioning them as we speak."

Delaney's mouth tightened. "I should have been there for that."

"No. You shouldn't have. You're exactly where you belong—safe and sound."

She dropped back, lying on the floor, and she stared at the ceiling. "But for how long?"

He'd asked himself that a hundred times while they were doing reports at police headquarters, and the only answer he could live with was *forever.* The shooting incident had hit too close to home in a lot of ways.

Because both of them needed it, Ryan touched her arm and rubbed gently.

She turned her head, glanced over at him and then at Patrick, who was between them. "So we just stay here, locked away, doing nothing?" she asked.

"We're doing something. We're waiting—where it's safe—and we're playing with Patrick. Personally, I can't think of a better way to spend the evening."

As if sensing he was now the center of attention, Patrick babbled some syllables. Kicked his legs. Gave a little grumble of protest. And rubbed his eyes again.

"It's his bedtime," Delaney said. She sat up and rolled her shoulders. "Mine, too. It's been a long day."

Ryan couldn't argue with her. The day had been so *eventful* that Delaney had seemingly forgotten he'd proposed to her in the limo. Or maybe she'd just intentionally pushed it out of her memory. The ploy wouldn't work. He'd remind her of his offer in the morning. Somehow he had to convince her that he would be part of Patrick's and her lives.

She stood, scooping up Patrick in her arms, and took him to the crib where she placed him on his side. He made a few more sounds of protest, which ended when Delaney turned on the cheery mobile. Patrick's sleepy gaze went right to it, and with his eyelids already lowering, he watched the tiny safari animals circle around to the music.

Ryan waited while Delaney went through

the ritual that was already becoming familiar to him. She kissed Patrick, murmuring something soft and soothing, and she rubbed his belly, her fingers moving in small, gentle circles.

"Maybe the police will have answers for us tomorrow," she whispered.

Her statement had a good-night ring to it, and Ryan decided she was both exhausted and probably wanted some time alone with Patrick.

Ryan obliged her. "See you in the morning." He kissed Patrick's cheek. Kissed hers, as well. And he headed back to finish up his calls.

He didn't shut the nursery door or the one to his office, so he could still hear the music coming from the mobile. Soothing, in a way. And in another way, it was a reminder that despite all his money, efforts and good intentions, he couldn't say with a one-hundred-percent certainty that Patrick was safe.

Neither was Delaney.

That put him face-to-face with all the old fears, and he cursed himself for getting too close to her. For wanting her.

And for needing her.

But while he cursed himself, Ryan knew there'd been no choice. Caring for Delaney seemed as natural as breathing.

He glanced down at his wedding ring. *You're already married,* she had accused. But she was wrong. He wasn't. Ryan could pinpoint the exact moment he'd no longer felt like a married man. It happened that night she'd visited him. Actually, it had happened the very moment he laid eyes on her, and he knew there was no going back.

Heck, he didn't want to go back.

Ryan tugged off his ring, opened his upper right desk drawer, and placed it next to Adam's picture. This had become his memory drawer. And it contained his past.

But right down the hall was his future. His son and his son's mother. That didn't mean he would forget Sandra and Adam. That would *never* happen. However, he wouldn't let their memory stop him from reaching for what he could have now. A life with Delaney and Patrick.

"You can put the ring back on," he heard Delaney say.

He raised his head and saw her standing in the doorway. She looked much like she had that evening of her first visit. Except tonight she wasn't drenched or shell-shocked. She wore a pair of pale green cotton lounging pajamas. Baggy and probably unappealing on anyone else. But not on Delaney.

"It's time to put it away," Ryan said. "*Past time.* Sandra would have never wanted me to die with her that day. And that's what I'd tried to do."

He shut the drawer. No booming thunder or slash of lightning to signal the closure. No dramatic cosmic or spiritual event of any kind. But Ryan knew it was the first real step he'd taken toward healing. "Sandra would have liked you, you know that?"

Delaney shook her head. "It doesn't seem as if we had much in common."

"You're wrong. You both had your priorities right. Family first. That's where I fell short. I measured my success by my investment portfolio and the number of businesses I accumulated."

Ryan wouldn't make that mistake again. He had enough money to last him several lifetimes, and he was already taking steps to restructure his company so he'd have more time to spend with Patrick.

If Delaney allowed it, that is.

Nature versus nurture aside, Patrick might be his biological son, but it was Delaney who was responsible for the happy, well-adjusted baby in the nursery.

"Is he asleep?" Ryan asked.

"Yes." She motioned toward his desk. "Do you have a surveillance monitor somewhere around? He's probably zonked out for the night, but I still like the idea of being able to check on him while we talk."

Ryan angled the computer screen so she could see it, and with a few clicks on the keyboard, they had a panoramic view of the nursery. Not just the crib. But every corner of the room.

"Thanks. I'm feeling overprotective these days." An understatement. Ryan could tell she was anxious and had something on her mind. Hence the *while we talk* comment.

She shut the door to his office quietly and walked to his desk. No heels clicking on the hardwood floor tonight. She was barefoot, her pink toenails peeking out from the bottom of the pj's. "I've been thinking about what you said in the limo, before the gunman opened fire."

Ryan was more than surprised that she'd

decided to bring it up. Especially since she'd avoided it all afternoon and evening. "About my marriage proposal?"

"Yes." She paused, pursed her lips. "I think you'll agree it's the worst idea you've ever had."

That stung a little. He certainly hadn't thought she would embrace the idea without an argument, but he hadn't expected a total dismissal, either. "It would solve a lot of our issues."

"So you've said. But it would also solve a lot if Patrick and I just stayed put. I mean, we're here already, and with the danger, there's no way I can go home. And you were right—we'll be safe."

She sounded convinced that it was the right solution. But her body language contradicted everything. She reached for her ring, probably to twist it, but instead put her hands behind her back.

"We're going to get the person responsible, Delaney. I promise you."

"I don't doubt it. I don't doubt *you*. But it might not happen anytime soon, and I can't risk Patrick's life by returning to my house." She huffed and glanced at the monitor. "Or by losing my temper and trying to barge in on an official interrogation."

"Glad you agree." Not that he would have let her anywhere near her father or Dr. Emmett Montgomery. The idea was to keep them as far away from Patrick and her as possible.

"That doesn't mean I won't talk to my father. You said it yourself—the P.I. spotted him on the very road where the shooting occurred. Maybe he was canvassing the place so he could find the right spot to ambush us."

That was Ryan's theory, too. Of course, it didn't rule out Keyes or Montgomery having done the same damn thing. Heck, there were times when he wondered if all three of them were in this together.

The lightning came without warning. A slash through the darkness and the rain. A vein of golden light. Followed by the thunder. He automatically turned away from the window. Nothing obvious. He didn't want Delaney to notice.

But she noticed anyway.

"Are you okay?"

He tried to toss it off with a shrug. "I don't care much for storms."

She walked to the window and looked out. "My mom didn't like them, either. Actually, they terrified her. When I was staying with her and one would hit, she'd cover her fear by trying to turn it into a party. Pizza. Popcorn. Ice cream. Lots of TV. Anything to keep her mind off it."

"Did it work?"

"Not for my mom. But since those were the rare occasions that she allowed me to eat junk food and watch TV, I didn't have the same reaction she did. For me, storms create a sense of anticipation. *Good* anticipation."

"Conditioned responses," he mumbled.

The security lights filtering through the rain-streaked windows created some interesting shadows. The shadows seemed to be streaming down her body, caressing her.

Or maybe he was simply projecting his own erotic thoughts.

Watching her, he started to project other thoughts, as well. Not sexual ones. But rather thoughts and concerns that dealt with security and potential gunmen lurking in the woods. Because he didn't like her standing in front of the window, Ryan caught her arm and eased her to the side.

His side.

Delaney studied their new positions, which likely violated her personal space, before she studied him. "You think the gunman might still be out there?"

"Not likely. But why take the risk?"

She stiffened, and her attention flew to the monitor. Probably to check and make sure Patrick's crib wasn't near a window. It wasn't. That wasn't by accident, either. It had been the top specification Ryan had given to Lena when he asked her to set up the nursery. Of course, at the time, he hadn't considered gunmen and rifles, but he hadn't wanted anyone to be able to observe their movements with long-range surveillance equipment. That was the very reason he hadn't taken Patrick and Delaney outside on the grounds.

Obviously satisfied that Patrick was all right, Delaney turned her attention back to him. "What conditioned you to dislike storms?"

Ryan almost told her. A mechanical response. But then, he realized it was no longer so mechanical, because, mingled with those horrific memories, were more recent ones. Of the stormy night of Delaney's first visit. And her presence now. That was the thing about memories and conditioned responses.

New ones could be made to erase the bad ones.

If he allowed them to be made, that is.

"Storms," she repeated, her voice whispery and tentative. "And the car accident where you lost your family. They're connected?"

He hadn't braced himself to hear the truth said aloud, and he almost backed away. But the look in her eyes grounded him. She seemed to be offering him a lot with those eyes.

Compassion.

Comfort.

A chance to break down a few more barriers.

Ryan hoped his voice held steady. "It was storming that afternoon."

She nodded. "That's why you were so uncomfortable the night you were driving me home."

"I didn't know it was obvious."

"It wasn't. But I noticed." She touched his arm lightly with just her fingertips.

Much as she'd done to Patrick while she was trying to get him to fall asleep.

It certainly didn't have that effect on Ryan.

The heat rolled through him.

She was no doubt feeling vulnerable and going through an adrenaline crash thanks to the shooting. Ryan could have probably talked himself out of touching her.

Probably.

But he didn't even want to try.

In the distance, still miles away, lightning speared through the sky again. Not one slash of light but several. Like a fireworks display put on by the gods. Thunder came as a soft continuous grumble, surrounding them.

She turned to him slowly, and he watched the lightning dance over her face. All those angles. The sensual curve of her mouth. He suddenly wanted to feel that mouth. To take it. And to know that it was his for the taking.

They waited a heartbeat, maybe to give the other a moment to reconsider. But the time for reconsidering was over.

Ryan reached for her, and she reciprocated. He couldn't have said who the winner was. Both, he decided when their mouths met. The need didn't surprise him. But, man, the energy did. Raw, pure energy. As if they'd been waiting for this a long time.

The jolt was instant.

No cool, gentle touch of lips. Not this. This was all fire, all need, and it moved in fast. Storming through him. Some unstoppable force that he didn't want to curb anyway. He wanted it to build until all of what he was feeling for her was sated.

Delaney obviously wanted that, too. She came up on her toes, plunging her body against his. Coiling her arms around him. Both of them grappled for position. And amid all that grappling, touching and caressing, Ryan's back hit the wall. Delaney landed against him.

Suddenly, everything was crystal clear. Razor sharp. Powerful and honed, like the spikes of lightning that tore through the distant sky. Everything was reduced to this one moment. To now. He wouldn't turn away from it. He wouldn't turn away from her.

She continued to kiss him. Not just his mouth but his cheek and his jaw, and then she took her mouth to his neck. A frantic pace. A whirlwind of energy. And all that energy was being released in the kisses.

Ryan responded. He had no choice about that. She was taking the firestorm already inside them and fueling it until the sensations were almost unbearable. Yet, he stood there and took everything. And wanted more. So much more.

"Make it count, Ryan." She spoke against his skin. Her mouth was on his neck. After yanking his shirt out of the waistband of his pants, her searching fingers delved underneath to his chest to explore.

"That's the plan."

She sought out every muscle. Every inch of warm, sweat-dampened skin, even the flat nipples buried in his chest hair, until the touching was no longer enough.

Her eyes were wild, and breath came out in short, hot bursts. That fed him in a way nothing else could, and he did some touching of his own. He slid his hand between them, over her left breast, and cupped her through her pj's top. She was full and firm. But touching her that way was not enough.

Not nearly enough.

"Now," she demanded.

Part of Ryan, a very specific part, was pleased with the demand. His body was begging him to take her. Right then, right there. To strip off the clothes that prevented him from really touching her. From really tasting her. He went with her suggestion and pulled open her top.

He didn't stop there.

Ryan located the front latch on her bra, flicked it open, and her breasts spilled into his hands.

She moaned. A purely feminine sound of pleasure. And like everything she'd done, it had an effect on him. It sent his heart pounding and his blood racing.

Their bodies came together. Bare chest against bare breasts. The feel was incredible, and it gave him plenty of ideas of what he wanted to do to her. But the idea that began to flash in his head was *take her now.*

So Ryan did something about that.

He turned, repositioning them. Delaney made a small sound of protest at the temporary loss of their body contact, but any further protest faded when he backed her against the wall.

And he touched her.

First, her breasts. Lightly stroking her nipples with his fingertips. He didn't stop there. He went lower. To her stomach. Firm but soft. Man, she was so soft.

"Yes," she murmured. Delaney dropped her head onto his shoulder, planting some kisses there. She fanned her fingers over his chest.

Ryan took a second to savor the sensation, but every inch of him was pressing to take more of her, which he did. He slid one hand to her backside. Slipping inside her pj's so he could cup her and press her harder and closer to him.

Delaney cooperated. And she gave her own personal spin on things. She not only pressed harder, she pressed harder in the right place. The soft folds of her body caressed him and nearly had him seeing stars.

Because her body caresses were making him crazy, Ryan eased his other hand down her stomach and lower. Inside her panties and into the fragile silk. His fingers found her. Wet and hot. Ready.

That stopped her sensual press against his body. Grasping him, she actually inched back a little so he could have his way with her. He made his way through the slick moisture. A long, lingering caress that brought on a shudder, an erotic hitch of her breath.

He wanted to feel her release, to see her face when she went over, so he continued to touch. To stroke. Deeper. Harder. She moved into the strokes. And she moved against him. Deeper this time though. Against his fingers, and against his body. A slow, sensual slide that brought out every basic, every carnal instinct inside him.

Ryan was sure she was close, that the strokes would take her over the edge. But Delaney obviously had something else in mind.

Her head whipped up, and she reached for his shoulders. Reversing their positions, she pushed him against the wall. While she didn't stop him from touching her in the most intimate way, she launched into some intimacies of her own.

She went after his zipper. And succeeded. No fumbling. She got it right the first time. Those agile fingers bypassed his boxers and slid right over his erection.

Ryan cursed and considered begging for

mercy. But it didn't seem as if she were in a mercy-giving mood. She obviously wanted him hot and fully aroused.

Which is exactly what he was.

"Enough of this," he grumbled.

He didn't even consider logic or logistics. He launched them forward. Most of her body landed on his desk, and he landed on her.

With his blood raging, and his heartbeat thundering, he dragged her pj's bottoms and panties off her. While he was doing that, Delaney freed him from his boxers. They didn't waste any time. Frantically, they latched on to each other. As if even a second was too long to be apart. It was with that same frantic energy that Ryan entered her. Sliding deep into the welcoming heat of her body.

"Yes," she whispered. Not just a sound of triumph. But more. Much more.

Ryan heard himself echo the same response, and for a too brief moment before the primal demands took over, he realized that everything about this, about her, was *yes*. Delaney was the opposite of barriers. The antithesis of the pain and sorrow he'd felt for so long.

She was his hope.

He couldn't hold back the need any longer so he began to move. To take them to the only place they wanted to go.

He captured her gaze, because he wanted to watch her. Ryan fought through the clawing need to claim and possess so he could see exactly what this did to her. It didn't matter that he felt his own body going over, as well.

Face-to-face. Body to body. Wet skin whispering against wet skin. Him, inside her. Moving. Clutching. Gripping. Sliding. To a frantic, feverish pace. Until neither of them could hold back any longer.

Ryan felt her surrender. Not with the desperate need they'd taken each other, but a gentle, sweet surrender.

"Ryan," she said.

Just his name.

And that was enough.

For him to let go and follow her.

"DID WE SURVIVE?" Delaney asked, and it wasn't a totally rhetorical question. Her body was still humming, and the whole experience with Ryan had been so wonderful, so incredible, that it had a dreamlike feel to it.

But yes, she was fairly certain they'd survived.

Ryan chuckled. Lazy and slow. The sound of an exhausted but satisfied man. He looked it. His hair was rumpled, as were his clothes, and he was smiling.

Delaney was sure she was doing some smiling of her own. She was damp with sweat, her heart was still racing, and her breath was minutes away from being level. Ryan's weight was still on her, a pleasant sensation in itself. But that pleasantness and the afterglow of great sex couldn't completely negate the reality that she was darn uncomfortable.

She fumbled beneath the small of her back and finally located the culprit responsible for her discomfort. A stapler remover.

"Sorry," Ryan mumbled. He lifted himself off her and caught her arm to help her up. "I should have taken you to bed."

Delaney glanced at the disarray on both the desk and them. "I doubt we would have made it. We were in a bit of a hurry." She winced at the cramp in her leg and located her pj's bottoms. She didn't bother putting on her underwear first. With that cramp, she'd probably fall. Not exactly the dignified end to a passionate bout of lovemaking. Instead, she slipped on her pj's and crammed her panties in her pocket.

Beside her, Ryan fixed his clothes. When he was done he slid his arm around her waist, hauled her to him and kissed her. Really kissed her. "Sleep with me."

Amused, she looked up at him. "I just did."

"No. *Sleep* with me. In my bed. So I can hold you all night."

Delaney realized she needed that probably almost as much as he did. She nodded.

That was the green light he'd apparently been waiting for, because he got her moving out of his office and to his bedroom. Delaney knew the way, since the nursery was sandwiched in between Ryan's and her suites. But with each step, the reality continued to emerge.

And that reality began to haunt her.

She stopped in the doorway of his room. It was impressive, as was the rest of his house. At least triple the size of a normal bedroom and tastefully decorated in monochromatic shades of pale green.

"I have a security monitor next to my

bed," he let her know. "So we'll still be able to keep an eye on Patrick." He stopped when she didn't enter, and looked back at her. "This wasn't mine and Sandra's room."

She hoped she didn't look too relieved. But she was. Delaney went to him. Into his arms. And he pulled her to the bed.

It felt perfect.

Well, almost.

His arms were warm and strong, and Delaney even felt comfort in the steady beating of his heart next to hers. But what she didn't feel was the certainty of what all of this meant. Ryan wanted her, she didn't doubt that, but he also wanted his son. And even though they'd just made love, she couldn't be sure that she was here in his bed because of their lovemaking.

And that made her wonder just how far Ryan would go to keep Patrick.

She didn't question the sincerity of what had just happened between them. No. He couldn't have faked that. But maybe he was lying to himself. Maybe he'd approached this as he approached many of his business deals. And in the ultimate scheme of things, he would definitely need to win her over to pave the way to keep his son.

In a sense, it was the most important deal he'd ever make.

"Don't doubt what just happened between us," he whispered, as if reading her mind. Or maybe he was simply reading her body language. Because she realized her muscles had tensed. He brushed a kiss on her forehead.

"I won't," she promised.

But Delaney knew in her heart that it wasn't true.

She did doubt it.

Heaven help her, she did.

Chapter Fourteen

While he waited for Quentin's call, Ryan sat at the desk in his office and went over his notes, again. Not that he was sure it would help to review their three suspects and the havoc that at least one of them had caused.

No. it probably wouldn't help.

But since neither the police nor Quentin had been able to find any physical evidence to link Richard Nash, Emmett Montgomery or Bryson Keyes to the attempts on Delaney's and his lives, then maybe he'd get lucky and find something in the notes he'd been compiling.

First, there was the road incident that had landed Delaney and him in the ditch. If Richard Nash had been following his daughter and had been upset about her visit to the estate, then he could have been enraged enough to cause what happened. Plus, he had no alibi.

But then, neither did Keyes or Montgomery.

Still considering that, Ryan got up from his desk and walked to the window. Other than a few puddles on the road, there was no sign of the storm that had hit the night before. A direct contrast to the storm going on inside him. His personal life seemed to be coming together.

Seemed to be.

But even with his doubts in that particular area, it was Delaney and Patrick's safety that was causing the emotional turbulence. Every second that he'd held Delaney in his arms, every moment of their night together, only made the turmoil worse. Because the more he cared about Patrick and her, the more he feared losing them.

The phone rang. Ryan was too antsy to stay seated, so he stood and pressed the speaker function.

"Good afternoon," Quentin greeted.

"Is it?" Ryan countered.

"I'd say so. We've got a solid lead on Dr. Keyes."

Finally.

"The police don't know about this lead yet," Quentin explained.

"Good." Ryan wanted first crack at him. "Where is he?"

"That's the not-so-good news, boss. Judging from the paper trail we picked up, he's at a hotel in downtown San Antonio. He appears to be draining his accounts so he can make a run for it. However, he just checked into the hotel last night. Before that, he was staying at Hideaway Lake."

Ryan was already reaching for his jacket, and for the Glock in his desk drawer, but the mention of that resort stopped him in mid-reach. And he cursed. Hideaway Lake was less than fifteen miles from his estate.

On the same side of his property where those shots had been fired.

"Don't even think about going after him," Quentin warned. "This is exactly what you pay me to do, and I'm already on the way to see him. Besides, there's no way you can question him objectively."

While the argument was good, it didn't convince Ryan to back off. Keyes probably had answers as to what was going on, and those were answers Ryan wanted. *Now.* He grabbed his jacket, shoulder holster and Glock.

At that exact second Delaney walked into his office.

Not alone, either.

She had Patrick with her.

During the short time she'd been at the estate, Ryan had learned that she was a casual-clothes kind of person. Today was no different. She had on well-worn snug jeans and a simple stretchy top that was the same tropical green as her eyes.

Eyes that showed a lot of fatigue.

The stress was no doubt catching up with her, even though she managed to eke out a smile.

"Did you hear me, boss?" Quentin asked. "*I* should be the one talking to Keyes. This isn't a good time for you to be out and about. You've got responsibilities there."

Since his security manager obviously didn't know that Delaney was in the room, listening, Quentin had no idea just how accurate and timely his remark was.

Hell.

Ryan shoved the Glock back into his

desk and draped his jacket over his chair.
This was not the time for a hot head. He
needed to stay calm. And he needed to be
at the estate. If he left to meet with Keyes,
he could be leaving both Patrick and Delaney in a more vulnerable position.

"Keep me posted, Quentin," Ryan instructed him, and he pressed the button to
end the call.

"You found Dr. Keyes?" Delaney immediately asked. She shifted Patrick from
her arms to her hip.

"Yes." Ryan left out the part about how
close Keyes had been. Too close. Which
meant the doctor had been in the proverbial catbird seat.

Close enough to strike.

And maybe the doctor had done just
that.

"So if Keyes is the one and Quentin can
get him to talk, this might all be over
soon," Delaney summarized.

Ryan settled for a nod, and because Patrick was fussing and squirming, he walked
to them.

Delaney handed Ryan a bottle. "I
thought you might like to feed him."

He eyed the bottle, his obviously hungry

son and even the blue bib Patrick was wearing with his overalls.

"Come on," she coaxed. She nudged Ryan toward his chair, had him sit and deposited Patrick into his arms. "It's a great way to get your mind off other things."

Patrick stared up at him. His son was obviously skeptical. He had a you-don't-have-a-clue-what-you're-doing look in his baby blues. The expression had Ryan smiling. And relaxing a little. He relaxed even more when he touched the bottle to his son's mouth. That was the only impetus Patrick needed to start gobbling down his afternoon meal.

It was a first. Feeding his son. Adam had never been quite healthy enough for Ryan to experience such things. And this experience put a lump in his throat.

"Thank you for this," Ryan told her.

"Don't thank me yet. Next on the list is diapering practice. He has a tendency to pee during the process, and his aim is remarkably good. Think the geyser at Yellowstone, and you'll have an idea of what you're up against."

Ryan pretended to be disgusted, but it

was yet another reason to thank Delaney. The feeding, the diapering, just the fact she was there with him now—she was including him in Patrick's life.

But not hers.

No.

Like Patrick, Ryan didn't have any trouble interpreting the look in her eyes.

After having wild sex with her on his desk, he'd thought Delaney and he were moving forward in their relationship. And it seemed that way when she accompanied him to his bed. But then in the morning, she'd pulled away. Heck, she was pulling away now. He could feel it despite the frequent smiles and the reassuring tone.

"Lena said you got a call from your father this morning," he commented.

"Oh. That." She propped her hip against the edge of his desk and stared down at Patrick. "Nothing to tell. Same old stuff. He's angry. He wants me to help him get revenge, and so on and so on."

"He's knows you're staying here?"

"He knows." She paused, blew out a weary breath. "I called an attorney a little while ago and asked him to look into the procedures for having my father's mental stability evaluated. That's the first step to having him committed."

It was a good first step, but it didn't solve their problems. Ryan needed Richard Nash out of the picture *now*. If Keyes or Montgomery was the culprit, he didn't want an irate Nash to join in either doctor's effort to do Delaney and him in.

Patrick grunted softly, kicked, and nudged Ryan's stomach with his elbow. That drew Ryan's attention back to him. His son was greedily drinking the milk, but some of it was streaming out of the corner of his mouth, down his chin and onto the sleeve of Ryan's shirt.

Delaney leaned in and used the corner of Patrick's bib to wipe it away. "Wait until next month when he starts eating rice cereal. He should be able to make a real mess with that. My advice? Stick to washable cotton clothes, or your dry-cleaning bill will skyrocket."

"Does that mean you'll be here next month?" But Ryan instantly regretted the question.

Delaney flinched.

"Sorry," he said. He waited to see if she

would reassure him that his apology wasn't necessary, but she was silent. "Do I also need to apologize for making love to you last night?"

"No." Thankfully, she said it quickly, and it sounded sincere. "Last night was wonderful. The best ever for me."

"But?"

She lifted her shoulder. "I know you're trying hard to make this work, but you're not in love with me, Ryan. No, don't," she added when he opened his mouth. To say what exactly, he didn't know. But Ryan wouldn't have let that comment stay too long between them.

Delaney pressed her fingers to his mouth. "That wasn't my way of trying to put you on the spot. Truth is, I don't really want to talk about it." She glanced down at Patrick and forced a smile. "You can put him down for his nap once he's finished. I need to get some work done while we wait to hear from Quentin."

She made it three steps to the door.

"You're not in love with me, either," Ryan pointed out.

She stopped and paused before she eased back around. Ryan was more than a little surprised by what he saw there. Not a quickly delivered agreement.

Perhaps not an agreement of any kind.

"Delaney?" he questioned.

She simply shook her head. Not necessarily a denial of her feelings though. "Everything is mixed up right now. It's best if we just back away from each other."

Ryan didn't agree, but he decided it wasn't a conversation he should have with Patrick in his arms. It would have to wait. But not for long.

The intercom buzzed a second before he heard Lena's voice. "You have visitors at the gate. It's Emmett Montgomery and Bryson Keyes, the doctors from the New Hope clinic."

Delaney pressed her hand to her chest, as if to steady her heart, before she hurried across the room and took Patrick. She also took the bottle so that Ryan could turn on the security feed.

There they were.

Dr. Emmett Montgomery was behind the wheel. Keyes was in the passenger seat. And Montgomery's face was almost the same gray color as his sleek car.

"Tell Mr. McCall it's urgent that I speak

to him," Montgomery said, his voice shaking. He fired several nervous glances around him.

"Well?" Lena asked. "Should the guards let them in?"

Ryan considered that, but it didn't take long for him to realize he didn't want either of the men anywhere on the estate. He was about to redirect the audio so he could tell them that, and question the two, but Montgomery beat him to the punch.

"Mr. McCall?" the doctor said, staring right into the surveillance camera. "You have to let us in. *Please.*"

Ryan started to answer, but Delaney beat him to it.

"And why would we want to do that?" she countered.

The doctor stared into the camera. "Because I have some information that you and Mr. McCall need to hear. I know who's trying to kill you."

With that, Montgomery turned his accusing gaze directly at Bryson Keyes.

DELANEY INSTINCTIVELY clutched Patrick closer to her chest. "Don't trust either of them," she warned Ryan.

He clicked off the audio transmission so that Montgomery and Keyes wouldn't be able to hear them. "There's not a chance of that."

But even while he was issuing the reassurance, Ryan was reaching for his jacket and his gun. That sent her stomach plummeting.

She put Patrick's bottle aside so she could catch Ryan's arm. "You're not going out there."

Her grip didn't stop him. He began to strap on a shoulder holster. "I need to find out what they know."

"Yes. And you can do that while you're inside here."

"Not likely." Ryan brought her hand to his mouth and brushed a kiss across her knuckles. No doubt meant to reassure her that what he was doing was okay. But it wasn't okay. "There are two armed guards, and they won't let Montgomery or Keyes inside the gate. Neither will I. They've gotten as close as they're going to get."

That was it. No room for argument. Which meant she wasn't going to be able to talk him out of this. Better yet, she didn't know if she should convince him to stay put. They did need answers, and Montgomery and Keyes were the people who could provide those answers.

Still, it was dangerous. Especially since Montgomery had made it seem like Keyes was the culprit. Still, why had Montgomery brought the man here? To *coax* a confession from him maybe?

Or maybe it was a trap, since the doctors could have been in on this together.

Ryan reached out and touched her cheek. "You said it yourself. We can't just stay locked away forever. We have to put a stop to what's happening."

He was right. Her brain knew that, but her heart was having a lot of trouble accepting it. She couldn't bear the thought of anything happening to Ryan.

"Swear to me you won't do anything stupid," Delaney said.

He looked at her directly. "I swear. But I'll ask the same of you. Stay put and don't go near the windows."

She nodded and clutched Patrick so tightly against her that he whimpered in protest. Delaney forced her arms to relax. No easy feat. Every muscle in her body had seemingly turned to iron.

"I'll be back," Ryan said. And that was her only warning before he headed for the door.

Delaney stepped in front of him. She opened her mouth, but nothing came out. Which made sense. Because she had no idea what to say to him.

Come back safe.

Be careful.

He already knew those things. They'd be unnecessary reminders and a waste of time. After all, there were no assurances that Montgomery would stay put. He could drive away before Ryan got to him.

"You can watch on the monitor," he added.

Another nod. Delaney felt her body start to tremble.

Ryan leaned in and kissed her. Then he kissed Patrick and that was it. He stepped around her and hurried to the door. This time, she didn't try to stop him. Nor did she say aloud the words that were pounding through her head.

I love you.

Heaven help her, she did.

The realization came not as an avalanche but as a soft whisper. A powerful one that she felt in her heart, her soul, every part of her.

She was in love with Ryan.

And she might lose him before she had a chance to tell him that.

Dreading what she might see, she cradled Patrick against her chest and went to the monitor. The doctors were still there sitting in the car on the other side of the gate. Montgomery was pleading with the guards to let them in. But not just pleading.

Begging.

"He tried to kill me," she heard Montgomery say. "Don't you understand?" He sounded on the verge of totally losing it.

A feeling that Delaney understood.

She took her attention from the doctor and looked past the gate. Past the guards. She could just make out the pastures that flanked the road. There were several potentially hot spots. Thick clumps of trees that could easily hide a gunman. Montgomery must have thought so, too, for he kept firing nervous glances at those clusters. Keyes, on the other hand, sat there quietly. His attention was fastened to the gate.

Patrick made a few grumbly syllables

so Delaney began to rock him in her arms, hoping he'd soon fall asleep. She added some soft shhs and hummed his favorite song. What she didn't do was take her attention from the monitor. Still no sign of Ryan, and she wasn't sure how long it would take him to drive from the house to the gate. Probably not long. Which meant he was only moments away from what could become a dangerous confrontation.

That didn't do much to steady her heart.

Neither did what Delaney saw on the monitor. One second, she had a clear picture of Montgomery, Keyes and the guards, and then there was a flurry of motion. Keyes moved. So did Montgomery and the guards, and she heard Montgomery yell something.

The screen went blank.

Delaney hadn't thought her heart could beat any faster, but that did it. She tapped the monitor, praying that it was just a temporary glitch. But the screen stayed empty.

She tried the computer itself, attempting to repeat the same keystrokes that Ryan had used to first get the video surveillance.

Nothing.

Since going to the window would be

stupid, she resisted that, but while still keeping a firm grip on Patrick, she fumbled around on the desk, looking for whatever device she needed to call for Lena. She didn't see an intercom, so she picked up the phone.

Picking it up was as far as she got.

Because something stopped her cold. The noise. Specifically, the blasts.

First one.

Then, another.

And a third.

Three thick jolts of sound that tore right through all of Ryan's promises and reassurances that he would be okay.

She instantly recognized the noise.

Someone had fired gunshots.

Chapter Fifteen

The sounds of the shots stopped Ryan cold.

He pulled his car to the side of the road, lowered the window and listened, hoping and praying he'd been mistaken about the sound.

All he heard was silence.

He was within a hundred yards or so of the gate, but because of the curvy road, he wasn't able to see the guards or either of the doctors. He almost called out to them, but his instincts told him that wasn't a good idea.

His instincts told him other things, as well.

That he wasn't going to like what he saw when he got to the gate.

Thank God, Delaney and Patrick were safe in the house, but Ryan was more than a little anxious to get back to them. Delaney was probably terrified. With good reason. She'd no doubt heard those shots. Plus, there had already been three attempts to kill them, and it was entirely possible that the shooter wanted another chance.

Because he couldn't risk making noise, he pressed 911 on the car phone and whispered, "I need the sheriff and an ambulance."

Other than his name and address, he didn't give any details, not that he had any to give at this point, but he knew the emergency operator would send the authorities out to the estate. Unfortunately, that wouldn't happen soon enough. The sheriff's office and the hospital were a good twenty minutes away.

A lot could happen in twenty minutes.

Ryan drew his weapon and got out of his car, easing his door shut so he wouldn't be heard, and ducked into the thick cover of the shrubs and trees. Hurrying now, he went toward the gate, all the while wondering what had gone wrong.

Had the two guards at the gate fired those shots? Montgomery, maybe? Or was it someone else? Like Delaney's father. Of course, it was also possible that Keyes had managed to wrestle the gun from Montgomery and was in the throes of a getaway.

Ryan stopped when he reached the last

curve before the gate, and peered through the low-hanging branches of an oak. He immediately spotted Montgomery's car. The driver's door was wide-open, and the engine was still running. What he didn't see was either of the doctors.

Nor the guards.

The two armed men should have been posted in or near the gatehouse, but neither was anywhere in sight.

And that sent a slam of adrenaline through him.

At least the gate was still shut tight, which meant whoever had fired those shots hadn't gained access to the estate.

Well, hopefully that's what it meant.

The shooter would have to be in great shape and pretty agile to climb the ten-foot-high gate that stretched across the road. Unless the person had gone over one of the pasture fences. However, that would have set off perimeter security. It wouldn't have been a silent alarm either but a full blast of sound, something Ryan would have certainly heard. Triggering that would have also caused an automatic lock-down of the house.

There was movement to his left, on the

opposite side of the road. He shifted his position, aiming his Glock in that direction, but all he saw was a pair of blue jays. Hardly the threat that his body had prepared him to face. But that didn't mean the threat wasn't there. Oh, no. It was definitely there. Something had gone terribly wrong with Keyes and Montgomery's visit.

Bracing his right wrist with his left hand, Ryan walked closer. His heart pounded faster, and an image of Delaney and his son raced through his head. He had to stop whatever had already been set into motion. He couldn't let the person behind this take it any further.

Staying off the road and amid the trees, Ryan went closer, and he listened for any sound to indicate the guards had control of the situation, perhaps crouched down waiting to return fire. With each step, the sense of dread got worse.

And then he saw the blood.

No small amount, either. There was a pool of it on the ground directly in front of the gatehouse entrance.

Dreading what he would see, Ryan went even closer. It would have been easy to let the blood capture his complete attention, but he couldn't let that happen. He forced himself to stay vigilant. He glanced all around him while he moved closer to the gate.

He spotted one of the guards slumped on the ground near the driver's side of Montgomery's car. Ryan cursed. The guard didn't appear to be breathing, and even if he were still alive, he was bleeding fast.

Ryan inched toward the fence, until he was able to peer inside the gatehouse. The second guard was there, on the floor, facedown. Probably dead, as well.

Hell.

What had happened here?

Frantically, he looked around for Montgomery and Keyes. The men were nowhere in sight, but Ryan did spot something else.

More blood.

It wasn't easy, because his heart was pounding and his body had geared up for a fight, but he forced himself to look more closely at what he'd found. The blood didn't appear to belong to the guards. In fact, it led away from them. Not a lot. Just drops.

My, God. Either Keyes or Montgomery

had been shot. But which one? And had the other one done the shooting?

Moving, staying close to the fence, Ryan followed the trail of blood. It led to the back of Montgomery's car. His first thought was that maybe one man had been wounded and then run into the pasture for cover. But Ryan kept looking. And he saw that the trail continued on the passenger's side.

It didn't stop there.

The dark maroon-colored drops led directly to the gate.

There was no blood on the gate itself, and that had Ryan's attention zooming in on the control panel located just inside the gatehouse.

He cursed again.

There were bloody fingerprints on the panel. Specifically on the very button that would have opened the gate. With that realization, he whipped around, his gun still aimed, and looked at the secondary control panel next to him. It was just inside the estate, anchored to a metal post, and it was something he often used when he'd let himself in and wanted to close the gate behind him.

There was more blood.

And that meant Keyes, Montgomery, or both, were on the grounds. They'd used the gate to gain entry and then likely slipped into the dense trees that lined the road. He'd probably driven right past them.

Ryan turned and broke into a run. He sprinted straight for the estate, and he prayed—God, he prayed—that the person who wanted them dead hadn't already made it to Delaney and Patrick.

DELANEY FRANTICALLY TRIED to access another security camera so she could see what was going on. Ryan had to be all right. He just had to be.

She glanced down at Patrick, to try to give him a reassuring smile. A smile she would have had to fake. But she soon realized the fake smile wasn't necessary. Patrick had thankfully fallen asleep.

Repositioning him in her arms, she continued to jab at the keyboard, hoping she'd find the right combination.

The scream stopped her.

It was a woman. Probably Lena, since it was Sunday and most of the staff had the day off. Lena was one of the few people in the entire house.

Delaney fought the urge to rush to the door to see if she could help. Because if she did that, it could endanger Patrick. Instead, she eased her sleeping son onto the rug beneath Ryan's desk and rifled through the drawers to see if she could find another gun, anything, that she could use as a weapon.

She heard the footsteps then. It didn't seem to be just one set, but two. And they were rushed. Someone was definitely in a hurry, and the footsteps were headed up the stairs.

Right in her direction.

She had to protect Patrick.

Delaney couldn't waste any more time looking for a weapon. She bolted away from the desk so she could shut and lock the office door. It wouldn't be much of a barrier against a gunman determined to get in, but at the moment the door was the only protection she had.

She reached for the doorknob, but that was as far as she got.

The first thing she saw was Lena's terrified, pallid face. Behind her was Emmett Montgomery. Not Keyes. Just Dr. Montgomery.

He had a gun pressed to Lena's head.

Montgomery shoved Lena forward, and the woman plummeted to the floor. "Get in the corner and stay there," he ordered.

Lena did as she was told, scrambling on all fours. Only after she was on the other side of the room did the man step inside. In the same motion, he repositioned his gun.

And he aimed it at Delaney.

She saw the gun, knew the danger. Worse, judging from the sheer determination in Montgomery's eyes, he was more than willing to kill her. But what stopped her heart in mid-beat was her fear of what Montgomery might have already done to Ryan.

"Where's Ryan?" she demanded, and she didn't cower. Not because she wasn't afraid. She was. Actually, she was terrified. But she couldn't just let him run over her. Since the door ploy hadn't worked, she was the only protection that Patrick had.

"I suspect Mr. McCall is out and about. Perhaps even following Keyes." His voice was calm, as was the rest of him. Obviously, he wasn't unnerved with holding her at gunpoint. "Which is the exact reason we have to hurry. I'd rather not have to kill McCall if you don't mind."

So Ryan was alive. Well, maybe. Unless Montgomery was lying, but Delaney refused to believe Ryan might be dead. No, he was alive, probably already on his way to help her.

At the thought, her heart skipped more than just one beat.

Oh, mercy. If Ryan came running in to do what he did best—come to the rescue—then Montgomery would probably shoot him. That upped the urgency, something Delaney hadn't thought possible. But she had to figure out a way to get the gun from Montgomery before he used it on Ryan.

There was also another problem. Keyes. Was he out there, leading Ryan on a wild-goose chase? Or worse, like Montgomery, did Keyes have murder on his mind?

"What do you want?" Delaney asked.

"Something that I'm betting you won't give willingly."

Patrick.

She staggered back. "I won't let you have him."

And, by God, she meant it.

She would not let this monster touch her son.

"Then I'm glad the decision isn't yours to make." He shifted the gun in Lena's direction when she moved slightly, gave her warning glare and turned the weapon back on Delaney. "Here's the deal, and it's the only deal I'm offering. Get your son and come with me. *Quietly.* In exchange, Ryan McCall will live."

The glance he aimed in Lena's direction suggested that she wasn't on his list of intended survivors. Probably because she'd seen his face and could identify him. In other words, he was eliminating witnesses.

Perhaps not just for this incident.

"This has to do with the cloning," Delaney said.

"Yes, it does. I can't leave evidence lying around. Or rather standing around. And, Ms. Nash, you and your son are potential evidence. It was a mistake to *borrow* DNA. I see that now. Get your baby, and let's go."

And if she went with him, Montgomery would kill both Patrick and her. If she refused, he'd do it anyway—and kill Ryan, too. She tried not to let the magnitude of that bring her to her knees. But it was the ultimate struggle. Just the thought of losing either of them had her wanting to strike out at the man who was threatening them. But while that might appease her survival instincts, it wouldn't be smart.

Not with Montgomery holding the gun.

If he killed her, Patrick wouldn't stand a chance of surviving.

"My son's in the nursery," Delaney lied. "I'll go get him." That would get Montgomery out of the same room as Patrick and Lena. It might also buy her some time until she figured out what to do.

"No," was Montgomery's answer. And he made her wait several excruciating seconds before telling her exactly what he meant. "The housekeeper will get the boy. You'll stay here, and if she doesn't return within forty-five seconds, I'll kill you and then go looking for her. Believe me, it won't be pretty if that happens. Because, you see, I'm a desperate man."

He used his gun to motion for Lena to

get up. But he didn't leave it at that. Montgomery repositioned himself just inside the doorway, probably so he could keep an eye on both Delaney and Lena when she went to the nursery. But Lena never made it out of the room.

From beneath Ryan's desk, Patrick stirred.

Just a whimper.

It was more than enough, however, to capture Emmett Montgomery's attention. His teeth came together, forming a natural scowl, and he grabbed Lena and slung her back into the corner.

"You disappoint me, Ms. Nash," he said, his voice chilling. "I'd planned to kill you elsewhere. Easier cleanup and all that, but why wait? Besides, you've given me no choice. You've made it clear that I can't trust you."

She opened her mouth to plead with him, to do whatever it took to keep him from Patrick. And while she considered what to say, she also considered what to do. Her options were practically nil, but she could throw herself at him and hope that would be enough to catch him off balance.

She didn't get a chance to do either.

"Delaney!" she heard Ryan call out. She also heard his footsteps as he barreled up the stairs.

Montgomery reacted. Fast. He turned in Ryan's direction.

And fired.

Chapter Sixteen

Ryan got a split-second glimpse of Emmett Montgomery, and his gun, before he
heard the shot. He reacted out of instinct.

A reaction that probably saved his life.

Ryan dove to the side, his shoulder
bashing into the stair railing. He ignored
the jarring impact and the pain and came
up, ready to return fire.

But he was too late.

Montgomery had already ducked inside
the office where Ryan had left Delaney
and Patrick. Where he'd told her to stay.
And she no doubt had.

Which meant both of them were in
danger.

The thought of losing them triggered the
flashbacks. Ryan forced the images aside.
He couldn't let Sandra and Adam's deaths

make him lose focus. There was nothing he could do to bring them back, nothing, but he sure as hell could do something to save Delaney and Patrick.

So Emmett Montgomery was the man responsible for all of this? Not that it surprised Ryan. After all, Montgomery was one of the top suspects. But then, so was Keyes, and Ryan had no idea where the man was. Dead perhaps, since Montgomery didn't appear to be injured, that blood trail no doubt belonged to Keyes, and Montgomery was probably the man responsible.

Montgomery had apparently initiated his own personal crime spree. A spree that would soon end, one way or another, especially considering the sheriff and probably Quentin were on the way.

Unfortunately, Ryan couldn't wait for backup.

He heard Patrick cry. It was little more than a fussy whimper, definitely not a cry of pain. But it was enough to get Ryan's heart pounding and his body moving. Keeping close to the stairs and with his gun ready, he crept up. One step at time. He kept his attention focused on the office door.

"Montgomery?" Ryan shouted. "Are you ready to bargain?"

"Not with you."

Ryan watched for shadows and listened for any sound or movement to indicate that Montgomery was about to dart out the door and fire another shot. If he did, Ryan intended to fire first.

He had too much at stake.

"Then what we have here is a standoff," Ryan said. "Because I won't let you hurt them."

"No?" Montgomery stepped out then.

But not alone.

He had Delaney positioned in front of him like a shield. Her back was against his chest. His gun pressed to her right temple.

Ryan froze.

And no matter how hard he fought, the nightmarish memories returned with a vengeance. So did the grief and the pain of losing his wife and son. If he tried to shoot Montgomery, he could end up hurting Delaney instead. It was too big a risk to take, and yet he had to risk something to get them out of this.

"Drop your gun, Mr. McCall," Montgomery ordered.

Ryan met Delaney's eyes for only a moment. It was all he could risk, since seeing the fear in her eyes would only distract him. With that brief glance, he tried to reassure her that he would do everything within his power to keep Patrick and her safe. But it wasn't everything within his power that was troubling Ryan. It was the things he couldn't control.

Like Montgomery and his gun.

"He said he's going to kill us," Delaney whispered.

Not said with fear. Her voice was low and dangerous. Ryan understood completely. Their child had been threatened by this man who could take everything that mattered away from them.

Patrick cried again, and Ryan heard Lena trying to soothe him. But that wasn't all he heard. In the distance, there were sirens. Montgomery obviously heard them too, because he turned his right ear to the sound and cursed.

"I said drop your gun," the doctor warned. "And if you think I'm bluffing, just ask Bryson Keyes. Oh, wait. You can't ask him because he's already dead in your hydrangeas." Montgomery jammed the gun harder against Delaney's temple, digging into her skin and causing her to gasp.

Rage slammed through Ryan. Hearing her gasp and seeing the pain on Delaney's face made him want to launch himself at Montgomery and tear the man limb from limb.

And in that moment, that one horrible moment, Ryan realized how important she was to him.

But had he realized it too late?

"Time's up," Montgomery taunted. "I have no plans to spend the rest of my life in jail."

And Ryan had no plans to die today. No plans for Patrick and Delaney to be hurt or worse.

Ryan met Delaney's eyes again. And in that look he tried to convey what he wanted her to do, which was get out of his way so he could go gun-to-gun with Everett Montgomery.

Yes, she mouthed.

Just yes. But it was the only green light he needed. Because Ryan was watching her so closely, he saw the muscles in her arms tighten. Just a second before she dropped to the ground.

Montgomery reacted, too.

He fired.

Straight at Ryan.

The bullet slammed into the railing right next to Ryan. Montgomery didn't stop there. He dropped, landing way too close to Delaney and reaiming his gun at Ryan.

Delaney kicked the man, her foot smashing against his arm. It was enough of a distraction for Ryan to come off the stairs and aim his own weapon. He kept his hand steady by thinking of Delaney, of Patrick, and of how he wouldn't—couldn't—lose them.

Ryan fired. The bullet slammed into Montgomery's right hand. The man howled in pain, and his gun went flying.

Delaney didn't waste any time. She scurried across the floor, seized his weapon and came up prepared to fire.

Montgomery held up his hands. An act of surrender. But the operative word was *act*. From all appearances, the doctor might be giving up, but Ryan didn't trust him.

"Go to Patrick," Ryan told Delaney while he kept his Glock aimed at Montgomery. "Make sure he's okay." And in doing so, it would get her away from the man who'd nearly succeeded in killing her.

Delaney hesitated, volleying uneasy looks between Montgomery and him.

"The sheriff will be here any minute," Ryan added, praying she would leave. "Then he can arrest this worthless excuse for a human being."

She nodded, clamped her teeth over her bottom lip and slowly got to her feet. She'd barely managed to stand upright and hadn't even gotten her balance when Montgomery lunged for her.

It seemed as if everything was happening in slow motion. Yet it all seemed fast, too. As if everything were spinning out of control. Ryan felt his finger tighten on the trigger. Pressure that he knew would deliver a shot. And this time, he shot to kill. A double tap of the trigger, and both shots hit their target.

Montgomery clutched his chest and fell forward, his body slumping on the top of the stairs.

Ryan waited, checking for any sign of life while he kept his Glock aimed at the man.

But Montgomery didn't move.

Delaney waited, too, until the sounds of the sirens were so close that Ryan figured the ambulance and the sheriff were already on the grounds.

"Is it over?" Lena called out. With Patrick cradled against her, she peered out from the doorway.

Delaney hurried to them. Her breath was gusting, and she stumbled, but somehow she made it to them, and she took Patrick from Lena. She pressed a flurry of kisses on Patrick's face.

Only then did Ryan move. Up the stairs. Past a lifeless Montgomery. He went to Delaney and Patrick, and he pulled them both into his arms.

Delaney's breath broke into a sob, and she buried her face against his shoulder. "It's over," she whispered.

Ryan held on to them and didn't let go.

Chapter Seventeen

With the phone pressed to her ear, De-10aney looked out the window and saw Ryan's car making its way up the road to the estate. Her heart did a little flip-flop. Not an unusual reaction. In fact, it was becoming somewhat routine. Whenever she saw him, her heart did the flippy thing and her breath vanished for a second or two.

Talk about a ridiculous response.

She smiled.

Actually, it was an incredible response. One that made her feel alive.

"Delaney," she heard her father say on the other end of the line. Not exactly a greeting, but at least he'd accepted her call. She hadn't been sure that he would.

"How are you, Dad?"

"How do you think I am? I'm in this

mental health prison where you had me sent."

"It's not a prison. I checked it out myself, and it's a very nice place with some of the best therapists in the state."

"I don't care how nice it is—don't expect me to forgive you for putting me here."

"Maybe not. But I wouldn't be able to forgive myself if I didn't get you some help. Dad, you *need* help."

He didn't say anything for several seconds. "I suppose you're getting on with your life now that Dr. Montgomery is out of the way?"

He wasn't just out of the way, he was dead. As was Dr. Keyes. According to the police, Keyes had been a hostage, and Montgomery had planned to frame him to take the blame for not only the guards' deaths but also Patrick's and hers. The police had even managed to find computer records to verify that Montgomery hadn't just assisted with the cloning, he'd been the instigator so he could be a pioneer in a field he was certain would one day be legal. He'd been behind all of it. Including the attempts to kill Ryan and her.

Montgomery had almost succeeded.

Delaney figured she could let that haunt her for the rest of her life, or she could try to put it into perspective. For all the bad Montgomery had done, he'd also been the one responsible for Patrick's birth, and in doing so, he had given Ryan back his son. Thankfully, he hadn't done *more* than that. The police had learned that Montgomery had successfully cloned only one embryo from Adam's DNA. One embryo, one baby. Montgomery's other attempts to clone babies had failed. That meant someone out there wouldn't have to go through what Ryan and she had.

She glanced at the split-screen monitor and saw that Patrick was still taking his afternoon nap. She also took another look out the window. Ryan had just parked in the side driveway. "Yes. I'm getting on with my life."

"And I suppose you're doing that with McCall?"

Well, it'd been over two weeks since Montgomery had tried to kill them, and her father was no longer a threat to himself or others. Yet she was still at Ryan's estate. Delaney hadn't sat down to analyze that, but she wasn't in a hurry to leave, and Ryan didn't appear to be in a hurry for her to go.

A no-pressure kind of arrangement.

Neither of them talked about it, which, of course, created a different kind of pressure. One that had caused her a few sleepless nights. Delaney had asked herself a thousand times how he felt about her, but she hadn't asked Ryan.

Nor had he volunteered it.

Pressure, indeed.

"I'm not sure how Ryan fits into my life yet," she admitted.

"That's fine and dandy," he said with a heavy dose of sarcasm. "Just don't expect me to ever like him."

"I don't expect that." But she didn't rule it out as a possibility. Once her father was better, he might be able to see the man behind the facade.

And there was an incredible man behind that facade.

"By the way, McCall rescinded the buyout of my company," he said, trying to sound grumpy. But for the first time in years, there was hope in his voice. "He gave it back to me."

Delaney had to speak around the lump in her throat. "Did he, now?"

"He did. It has conditions, though. He'll continue to manage it until I'm out of this place, which might not be for months." He paused. "Tell him I said thanks."

"You can tell him yourself when you're better."

"Maybe."

That "maybe" was a huge leap for her father. One that Delaney thought might never happen.

She glanced out the window again, saw Ryan exit his car and immediately became alarmed when she noticed that his clothes were dirty. "Dad, I have to go. I'll call you soon."

"Do that. I'd like to hear from you every now and then. If you're not too busy."

That caused her to smile again, but it was short-lived when she got another look at Ryan. His clothes weren't just dirty, they were covered with mud.

He was covered with mud.

She tossed aside the phone and hurried out of her suite and down the stairs. She made it to the foyer just as Ryan opened the door and stepped in. He brought in a significant amount of mud with him.

Delaney went to him, immediately checking for injuries, but she didn't see any. Out of relief, she kissed him, mud and all.

"If I get a welcome like that," he drawled, "I'll have to get dirty more often." He slid his arm around her waist and led her back up the stairs.

The drawling and the smile he flashed didn't relieve her concerns. "What happened?"

He shrugged. "I had a crew combing the irrigation ditch with some highly sensitive metal detectors, and I decided to help them out." He stopped, opened his hand, and in the center of his grimy palm she saw the tiny butterfly charm that she'd lost from her ring.

Her heart and stomach did another flip-flop. "You actually found it?"

He nodded. "I thought about buying you another one, but it wouldn't be the same. So we've been sifting through pounds of mud and water since early this morning. I now totally understand the needle-in-a-haystack analogy."

And here she'd thought he was working at his office in San Antonio.

It wasn't the fact he'd found the butterfly that tugged at her heart, it was that Ryan had gone through so much trouble to search for it.

"Thank you," she managed to say, but it seemed inadequate.

With his arm still around her waist, he led her to his suite. "I need a shower. Care to join me?"

Perhaps because he thought she needed some coaxing, he planted a kiss on her cheek. Then her mouth. And he followed it up with a rather well-placed kiss to an extremely sensitive spot on her neck. In the past two weeks she'd learned that Ryan was very good at not only locating her erogenous zones, he knew what to do with them.

"Well, Patrick should be asleep for another hour or so." Delaney leaned into the neck kisses, leaned into him, and that unbalanced them. They practically fell through the doorway of his suite.

Ryan saved her by taking the brunt of the impact. While they were still wrapped around each other, he turned, his back landing against the wall. In the same motion, he kicked the door shut.

"I'll take that as a yes," he mumbled.

It was definitely a yes, and those kisses were already causing her to burn. Delaney went after his clothes. No finesse. Since the shirt was no doubt ruined away, she jerked open the front and sent buttons and thread flying.

Ryan didn't bother with finesse, either. As if ravaged with need, he stripped off her clothes, lifted her and wrapped her legs around his waist. He pressed her back to the wall. He entered her slowly. Too slowly. Delaney wanted hard and fast, but he actually stopped and looked at her.

"This is right. You know that, don't you?" he asked.

"Yes. Definitely, yes."

He brushed her hair away from her eyes. "I don't just mean the sex. Don't get me wrong—it's great. But there's more between us than this. Think about that for the next couple of minutes."

But she couldn't think about anything except the fact Ryan was inside her and moving exactly the way she wanted him to move. It was deep. It was perfect. But then he slowed just when he had her so close to the brink she could taste it.

"How do you feel about me?" he asked.

Ryan started to move again, the right way. Her mind turned to mush, and she was suddenly so close again. A few more of those well-delivered strokes, and she would—

He put his mouth next to her ear. "I love you, Delaney."

That did it. Her mind registered brief shock. Very brief. Then Ryan sent her spinning out of control to a place where words weren't even possible. She clung to him. He latched on to her. And they went over the edge together.

For several long moments the only sounds were their heavy, rushed breaths. He pulled back slightly and looked at her.

Somehow, Delaney managed to smile. "I love you, too."

The corner of his mouth lifted. "Do you really?"

"Mercy, yes."

"Is it because of the butterfly?"

"No. I was in love with you before you found it. That just sealed the deal."

The lifted corner of his mouth turned into a smile. "This calls for a celebration."

She glanced down at where they were still intimately joined. "I think we just did that."

He eased her to a standing position. "We can do a whole lot better than that."

"Well, even if we can't, it'll be fun trying."

"While I admire your insatiability, I had something else in mind." He picked up her clothes and handed them to her. "I want you to marry me."

"Marry you?" she repeated, her breath still choppy. If she thought the sight of him could flip-flop her heart, that was minor compared to this.

He put his fingers to her mouth to stop her from saying more. "For the record, I'm not asking you to marry me because of Patrick, because you're his mother and because I'm his father. That's not the reason I fell in love with you."

She eased his hand away. "It's not?"

"No. It's because you make me a better man. A whole man. You've told me a couple of times that I've jumped in and saved you. Well, you saved me, too, Delaney. And you didn't just save my life. You saved *me*."

Okay, that did it. She felt the tears and couldn't stop them. Didn't want to stop them. Because these were tears of happiness.

Ryan circled his arm around her waist and pulled her back to him. "So what do you say? Will you marry me?"

He didn't let her answer right away though. Ryan kissed her. Until she was breathless. Until Delaney could manage to say only one word. But it was the only word that mattered.

"Yes."

* * * * *

Don't miss Delores Fossen's next Harlequin Intrigue, coming in January 2006!

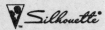

INTIMATE MOMENTS™

Sparked by danger, fueled by passion!

Passion.
Adventure.
Excitement.

**Enter a world that's
larger than life, where
men and women overcome
life's greatest odds for
the ultimate prize: love.
Nonstop excitement is
closer than you think...in
Silhouette Intimate Moments!**

Visit Silhouette Books at www.eHarlequin.com